"Why this cha
Who are you trying to hurt?"

Alex paused. "Me? What is it they say about a woman scorned?"

Isabel knew another surge of fury at his arrogance. "Oh, Alex. How you deceive yourself!"

An unidentifiable emotion crossed his face. "I came here to try and salvage something from the mess my grandmother created when she left you her shares. Will you consider being reasonable and selling them back into the family?"

"How reasonable was your uncle?" she spat angrily.

"I suggest you inform my uncle of your decision," Alex declared grimly, walking toward the door. Impulsively Isabel went after him.

"Daren't you wait for my answer yourself," she taunted.

Alex halted "Get out of my way!"

"Make me," she urged and it was only later that she realised how reckless her invitation had been.

ANNE MATHER began her career by writing the kind of book she likes to read—romance. Married, with two teenage children, this northern England author has become a favorite with readers of romance fiction the world over—her books have been translated into many languages and are read in countless countries. Since her first novel was published in 1970, Anne Mather has written more than eightly romances, of which over ninety million copies have been sold!

Books by Anne Mather

STORMSPELL
WILD CONCERTO
HIDDEN IN THE FLAME
THE LONGEST PLEASURE

HARLEQUIN PRESENTS

586—AN ELUSIVE DESIRE
610—CAGE OF SHADOWS
626—GREEN LIGHTNING
683—SIROCCO
715—MOONDRIFT
810—ACT OF POSSESSION
843—STOLEN SUMMER
869—PALE ORCHID
899—AN ALL-CONSUMING PASSION
1003—NIGHT HEAT

HARLEQUIN ROMANCE

1631—MASQUERADE
1656—AUTUMN OF THE WITCH

Don't miss any of our special offers. Write to us at the following address for information on our newest releases.

Harlequin Reader Service
901 Fuhrmann Blvd., P.O. Box 1397, Buffalo, NY 14240
Canadian address: P.O. Box 603,
Fort Erie, Ont. L2A 5X3

ANNE MATHER

burning inheritance

Harlequin Books

TORONTO • NEW YORK • LONDON
AMSTERDAM • PARIS • SYDNEY • HAMBURG
STOCKHOLM • ATHENS • TOKYO • MILAN

Harlequin Presents first edition January 1988
ISBN 0-373-11044-8

Original hardcover edition published in 1987
by Mills & Boon Limited

CHAPTER ONE

'THE OLD girl must have been senile!' declared Robert Seton angrily.

'But she wasn't,' countered his nephew, from the depths of an Italian leather armchair. 'Vinnie made quite sure you couldn't level that charge at her. She was perfectly sane when she made her will. And there are three medical affidavits to prove it.'

'I don't need reminding of that fact,' retorted Robert Seton irritably. 'I was merely voicing my opinion, that's all. An opinion which will be shared by a majority of the shareholders. For God's sake, Alex, leaving her interest in the company to Isabel Ashley! Is that really the behaviour of a rational human being?'

'Vinnie evidently thought so,' remarked Alex, pushing his hands into the pockets of his trousers and stretching his long legs out in front of him. 'She always did have a soft spot for Isabel. I suppose she saw this as a way of redressing the balance.'

'What balance?' His uncle was impatient. 'Isabel left this family with no more and no less than she came into it.'

Alex shrugged. 'Perhaps Vinnie didn't consider that was a particularly fair arrangement.'

'What are you trying to say, Alex?' Robert Seton gazed incredulously at the younger man. 'Do you agree with her philanthropy? I wouldn't have thought——'

'Someone has to play devil's advocate,' Alex overrode him smoothly. But then, as if a little of his uncle's agitation was rubbing off on him, he rose abruptly to his feet. 'After all, if you are going to oppose Isabel's admission to the board——'

'Which I am!'

'—you should consider all the alternatives.'

His uncle snorted. 'There are times, Alex, when that legalistic logic of yours infuriates me. The girl's an opportunist, for heaven's sake! Anyone can see that.' He pressed the balled fist of one hand into the opened palm of the other. 'I should have forbidden Vinnie to see her. I'll never forgive myself for allowing this to happen.'

Alex raised one dark eyebrow, as if doubting his uncle's ability to have forbidden Vinnie to do anything, before leaving him and strolling lazily over to the long windows. With his back to the room, he allowed the tranquillity of the scene beyond the leaded panes to soothe him. His grandmother was dead, after all. And he refused to let his uncle's ugly mood destroy the grief that still lingered.

Outside, the shadows were lengthening across gardens burgeoning with the growth of early summer. The lavish flower beds which Deacon, his uncle's gardener, tended so lovingly, provided a natural frame for lawns as green and well-kept as a bowling green, and the shrubs that marked their borders were as luxuriant as the rest. Deacon had green fingers. It was a well-known fact. And Alex could remember, when he was about six years old, being puzzled because the gardener's hands didn't look any different from anyone else's.

Beyond the perimeter fence, the tree-strewn parkland of the Denby estate stretched towards Peale Bay, and the estuary of the River Naze, which marked the eastern boundary of Denby land. *Seton* land, Alex supposed it was now, with sudden irony. His grandmother's death had marked the passing of the last surviving member of his mother's family. Virginia Denby had outlived both her daughters by some twenty years, but at the age of seventy-seven, she had finally lost the battle. He would miss her. Much more than he had perhaps realised. She had been such a dauntless old lady, and he had loved her very much. For twenty years, she had tried to fill the gap left by his parents' death, and throughout his teens and early manhood, she had been the recipient of all his confidences.

A fold in the downs hid all but a triangle of the sea from view, but the rolling fields and pasture land more than made up for this omission. This was the place where he had been born, where he and his cousin Christopher had played as children, and even though he now had a place of his own in London, he still regarded Nazeby as his home.

'You'll have to go and see her,' announced his uncle from behind him, and Alex turned disbelievingly to face his irate relative.

'Me!' he exclaimed ungrammatically. 'Oh, no. You have to be joking! If you want to get in touch with Isabel Ashley, do it yourself.'

'No, I can't.' Robert Seton made a sound of annoyance. And then, changing his tone, he added wheedlingly, 'You know she always blamed me for breaking up the marriage. If I were to go and see her, she'd probably laugh in my face. You know what kind of woman she is. If she thought that by holding on to those shares, she'd be dealing a blow to Denby Industries—*at me!*—she'd never agree to sell!'

Alex had to acknowledge that there was some truth in what his uncle was saying. Not to put too fine a point upon it, Isabel had disliked Robert Seton intensely, and she had accused him of turning Chris against her. Nevertheless, Alex had no intention of getting involved in any vendetta against the woman.

He had his own reasons for despising Isabel Ashley, and nothing his uncle could say would persuade him to act as his emissary. Let the company lawyers do it. There were enough of them, heaven knew.

'Why don't you send Chris to see her?' he enquired now, his lean, intelligent face taking on a distinctly sardonic expression, and his uncle swore.

'Are you mad?' The older man clenched his fists. 'Don't you know your cousin still harbours some kind of feeling for her? Haven't I been the unwilling recipient of his maudlin self-recriminations, when he's been in his cups? For pity's sake, Alex, the last thing I need is for that woman to get her claws into him again. He got out of a difficult situation once, but I wouldn't trust him to be so lucky a second time.'

Alex felt a growing tension in his neck, and tilted his head to relieve it. 'You can't expect me to do your dirty work, Uncle,' he declared flatly. 'If you want to deal with this matter impersonally, get John Frazer or Malcolm Stansfield to handle it. That's what they're paid for. I'm not.'

'You could be.' Robert Seton jumped at the possibility. 'Alex, you know it was your grandmother's dearest wish that you should be a part of the company. Do you think she'd have left those shares to Isabel if she'd thought she could have persuaded you to take a less than half-hearted interest in Denby Industries? Look, I'll make a deal with you. You persuade Isabel to sell, and you can have the shares. Nothing would give me greater pleasure than for you to take Vinnie's seat on the board.'

'No.'

Alex's refusal was polite but firm, and his uncle gazed at him frustratedly. For five years now, ever since Alex left bar school and latterly set up his own tax consultancy agency in London, Robert had been trying to persuade him to join Denbys, but all to no avail. So far as Alex was concerned, his cousin Christopher was his uncle's natural successor and, in spite of the close family relationship, Alex preferred to remain independent.

'It doesn't occur to you that it's what your mother would have wanted you to do, does it?' his uncle persisted now. 'I know she was your grandmother's younger daughter, and I know your father wasn't interested in making money, but, dammit, Alex, he was my brother, and when he crashed the car that killed the three of them, my wife included, that changed the situation somewhat, didn't it?'

Alex's jaw hardened. 'I'm not unmindful of the debt I owe to you and Vinnie,' he declared flatly. 'And if it's family loyalty you're calling in——'

'I'm not.' As if realising he might have gone too far, Robert swiftly interrupted him. 'Alex, Alex, you must know that you're the son I always wished I had. No—don't interrupt. It's true. You're like me. We think alike. I sometimes think there's more of me in you than there is in Chris! He's his mother's son. A Denby through and through. That's how the family fell on hard times, for heaven's sake! Because they bred generation after generation of milk-and-water thoroughbreds, without a shred of honest muscle in them!'

'Vinnie was a Denby,' pointed out Alex harshly, but his uncle scarcely paused in his stride.

'Only by marriage, Alex; only by marriage,' he retorted fiercely. 'And we'll never know what my wife and your mother might have made of the company because they're dead! But we're alive, Alex. You and I, we could make Denby's an international concern. We're already involved in the Brazilian mining operation, but I've got my sights set on Canada and the United States. With you behind me, to run the operation here, I'd be free to travel the world in pursuit of contracts. Denby Textiles is no longer the corner-stone of our operation. Denby Engineering and Denby Electronics outstripped it years ago. I want you with me, Alex, you know that. I dread to think what will happen to Denby's when Chris takes over. And he will do one day, Alex, unless you've got the guts to take it from him!'

Alex's face was grim. 'Chris is your son, Uncle Robert!' he exclaimed angrily, but the older man was not dismayed.

'So what?' he inquired indifferently. 'I'm not saying that I don't love him. I do. He's my only child, and I care for him deeply. But that doesn't mean I can't see his faults, and despair of them. Chris isn't cut out to be the next managing director of Denby's, Alex. You are. And you know it!'

Alex drove back to London later that night. As the sleek grey Ferrari covered the miles between Nazeby and his own house in Eaton Mews, he had plenty of time to go over what his uncle had said and he eventually decided, with some irritation, that Robert Seton would go to any lengths to get his own way. Not that Alex entirely disagreed with what his uncle had said. Chris would find it hard to apply himself to a real job, when the time came. For the past eight years, he had done little more than spend some of the vast sums of money his father's companies were making, and although he played around a bit as trouble-shooter for the organisation, his main source of enjoyment came from gambling. Even so, Alex had never considered his Denby heritage as giving him any claim on the company. When Robert Seton married his mother's sister, the textile trade was failing and, without Robert's business expertise, Nazeby itself might have had to be put on the market to help pay the company's debts. It was Robert's skill which had turned a losing concern into a thriving industry, and it was only fair that his son should inherit its advantages. Besides which, Alex had always wanted to be independent. He had never been content to bask in the glow of his uncle's generosity, and while Chris was getting sent down from Oxford and wasting his time at clubs and race tracks, Alex had gained a first in law. He could have done almost anything. He was offered jobs by friends of his uncle, other members of the business and banking community, but he had chosen to go to bar school. Then, instead of going on and becoming a famous barrister, as everyone had expected, he had entered a firm of tax consultants and spent the next three years learning what there was to know about income tax, and company tax, and all the other vagaries of the British tax system. In consequence, when he was twenty-six, he was able to set up on his own, and now, at twenty-nine, he owned a very successful company, the rewards of which were quite sufficient to satisfy his needs. It was the knowledge of this that made it comparatively easy to reject his uncle's proposition. He had no burning desire to be the newest director of Denby Industries, and if it meant seeing Isabel Ashley again, nothing could persuade him. Or so he thought.

Ten days later, he had reason to revise his opinion. A telex from New York was waiting for him at his office, when he arrived back from a late lunch, the gist of which sent him rapidly to the telephone.

'What's going on?' he demanded of his uncle's secretary, who had accompanied Robert on his trip. 'I have a message here, which reads: *See Ashley immediately, re sale of Denby shares.* My uncle knows I refused to handle this commission days ago. What game is he playing now? Is he there? Let me speak to him.'

'Mr Seton is in a meeting, and can't be disturbed,'

said Joan Ferris at once, and Alex's mouth compressed at the age-old excuse. 'He thought you might ring, and he asked me to tell you, the situation's changed. Apparently, Miss Ashley does want to dispose of her shares, after all. And as your uncle is out of the country at the moment, he's hoping you'll act as family mediator in his absence.'

'What's wrong with the solicitors handling it?' asked Alex flatly, his suspicions aroused. If Robert had thought he might ring, then why hadn't his uncle done the same? Sending a telex was so impersonal, and it gave Alex little room for manoeuvre.

'Mr Seton was sure you would understand that in a matter as delicate as this, a member of the family should be involved——'

'But not Chris,' Alex interrupted her harshly. 'OK, Joan, but I'll have something pretty strong to say to your boss when next I get hold of him. You can tell him from me, I don't appreciate his methods!'

'But you'll do it?'

'Do I have a choice?' Alex took a grudging breath. 'All right, Joan. You can leave it with me. But don't be surprised if I blow it. I'm not exactly in the mood to be tactful.'

It was not until Alex got back to his own house that night that he allowed himself to give any thought to his uncle's request. His profession entailed seeing clients at all hours of the day and night, and his evening had already been planned before he received his uncle's telex. In consequence, he had been able to put any serious consideration of what he had committed himself to to the back of his mind, and it wasn't until he was undressing for bed that its full import struck him.

It was annoying, because he had had quite a pleasant evening, dining with Howard Marsden and his wife. He had even succeeded in foiling Hilary Marsden's not-unsubtle efforts to attract him, and for once her rather obvious contempt for her husband's feelings had failed to arouse his impatience. Instead, he had concentrated his attention on the problem of Howard's particular tax liability, and he had not even been aware he had been avoiding thoughts of Isabel until the realisation came to him.

Unbuttoning his shirt, and pulling it free of his trousers, he regarded his reflection without liking. It was infuriating that the thought of his cousin's ex-wife should still have the power to disturb him, and he felt a renewed sense of resentment towards his uncle for putting him in his present position. If it wasn't for the affection he genuinely had for Robert, he could even now wash his hands of the affair and let someone else do it. But he had given his word, and was loath to break it, particularly if it meant restoring his grandmother's shares to their rightful branch of the family.

Nevertheless, he took a shower before getting into bed, letting the brittle spray pummel his body and run almost cold before turning it off. Then with a towel wrapped carelessly about his waist, he walked back into his bedroom, using a second towel to dry his hair before shedding them both on to the carpet.

He was tying the belt of a cream silk dressing-gown when he heard a knock at his door. At his resigned summons, a middle-aged man with greying hair put his head into the room, smiling somewhat diffidently at Alex's look of enquiry.

'I wondered if you'd be wanting a drink or a sandwich, perhaps,' he remarked ruefully, widening the door to reveal a small, wiry frame, dressed in a dark woollen dressing-gown over blue and white striped winceyette pyjamas. 'Sure, I was getting ready for bed, and I thought to myself, that's Mr Alex home already, if I'm not mistaken, and maybe feeling a bit peckish, if he's had an early dinner.'

'No, thanks, Kerry.' Alex regarded the cheerful Irishman with reluctant humour. For the past six years, ever since he had had his own establishment, Kerry O'Flynn had looked after him, seconded from the staff at Nazeby at Robert Seton's insistence. 'I don't need anything,' he added wryly, aware of the butler's darting gaze. 'And before you ask, I don't intend to leave those towels to dampen the carpet. I'll put them in the basket in the bathroom before I go to bed. I promise.'

'Now, would I be leaving you to clear your towels away?' demanded Kerry indignantly. Advancing into the room, he gathered up the two offending articles and tucked them under his arm. 'I'll be putting these in the wash tub, first thing in the morning. Like as not, before you're awake, unless you've an early call.'

Alex forced a thin smile. 'Thank you.'

'It's no trouble.' Kerry took his duties very seriously. 'Now, you're sure you've everything you need?'

'Everything.'

'Good enough.' Kerry backed out of the door. 'Then, I'll wish you a good night, sir. You take it easy. You're looking a little tired.'

'Am I?'

But Alex saved his comment until the inquisitive Irishman had closed the door behind him. Then, he walked into his dressing-room and examined his face more closely in the mirror above the hand-basin. It was true, he reflected sourly. The number of nights he had spent working recently were beginning to make their mark. And he'd had some trouble sleeping since his grandmother's will was published.

Grimacing, he rubbed his hand along the darkening curve of his jaw-line. He needed a shave, but what the hell! That could wait. It wasn't as if Penny was here to complain about his designer stubble. She wasn't due back from Kuwait until the beginning of next week and by then the upcoming interview with Isabel, which was making him so irritable, would be behind him.

He had his secretary ring her number, as soon as he arrived at his office the following morning. The sooner he dealt with the matter, the better, he had decided grimly, after spending another restless night. He had too much work on at the moment to prolong the aggravation.

He went into his own office while his secretary made the call, refusing to speculate on the reasons why he could recite Isabel Ashley's phone number from memory. Absorbing the reassuringly familiar atmosphere, he spent the next few minutes flicking through the mail on his desk, only pressing the intercom when it seemed the girl was taking an inordinately long time to make the connection.

'I'm sorry, Alex,' Diana Laurence apologised, when she came on the line. 'But there's no reply from Miss Ashley's number. Do you want me to try somewhere else?'

'Oh——' Alex swore somewhat colourfully, and then, quickly recovering himself, he added, 'I'm sorry. And no, I don't have another number for Miss Ashley.' He sighed. 'Leave it for now, will you, Diana? I'll get back to it later.'

'Very well.'

Diana had been with him too long to be offended by his outburst, but after she had rung off, Alex flung himself irritably into the leather diplomat chair at his desk. He could have given her an alternative number. He knew that eighteen months ago Isabel had joined the Ferry agency, and it would have been a simple matter to call Jason Ferry and have him locate Isabel for him. But that would have meant showing his hand to someone else besides Isabel, and he had no desire to advertise his mission. *Mission Impossible,* he thought glumly. He just hoped she hadn't gone off on some overseas assignment.

Diana rang just then to let him know that his first appointment of the day had arrived, and realising he could not allow his frustration with Isabel Ashley to interfere with his work, he had her send the man in. What else could he do, after all? He would have to ring Isabel this evening. If, at that time, there was still no reply, he'd be perfectly at liberty to tell Robert that he hadn't been able to reach her.

He had lunch with a graduate friend from Oxford, and he was quite glad that his afternoon was taken up with visiting a co-operative in East London. It was a free service he offered, in conjunction with a government-backed grant scheme, and the group presently running the small engineering company were more than willing to show him over the workshop. They wanted his advice about tax allowances, and his opinion concerning how much they could afford to invest in new machinery.

'I bet that piece of machinery cost more than we'll make this year,' commented Brenda Jeffries, one of the technical trainees, who had taken over the paperwork, admiring Alex's Ferrari from the window of the first floor office. 'And you know,' she added, turning so that he could appreciate her profile, 'I bet someone like you doesn't need a car to pull the birds. I don't suppose you need an assistant, do you, Mr Seton? I have had—secretarial experience.'

'I'm sure you have,' Alex responded humorously, fitting his papers back into his briefcase. 'And if I discover we have a vacancy, I'll keep you in mind.'

'You will?' Brenda's round blue eyes sparkled. 'I'll remind you of that next time you come.'

'OK.' Alex walked towards the door. 'Just don't forget to tell Ted Ripley I'll be in touch, hmm? G'bye.'

''Bye.'

Brenda bestowed another wistful smile, and Alex's lips were twitching as he descended the flight of iron stairs to the yard below.

But driving back to his office, his humour dissipated. 'Try that number again, will you, Diana?' he requested, as he crossed her office to his own, and then gritted his teeth impatiently when she asked, 'Which number?'

'Isabel Ashley's, of course,' he retorted, and then, realising how unreasonable he was being, he sighed. 'I'm sorry. It's been a long day. Did you take a note of the number? It's——'

'I have it here,' said Diana, unperturbed. 'Oh—and I've left some messages on your desk. Your cousin, Chris, has been ringing you on and off all afternoon.'

'Chris?' Alex suppressed a groan. That was all he needed, for Chris to find out he was trying to see Isabel. In spite of his opposition to his uncle's request, he had to agree with Robert that Chris's seeing his ex-wife again was not a desirable proposition. 'What did you tell him?'

'That you were out at Walthamstow, of course,' said Diana, pressing the buttons that made up Isabel's number. She smiled up at him. 'It's ringing now. Do you want to take it?'

Alex hesitated, and then shook his head. 'I'll wait,' he said, suddenly convinced that Isabel would not be there. Nothing short of a personal confrontation was going to resolve this situation; he could feel it in his bones.

But, amazingly, after a few moments, he heard the connection being made, and Diana looked up at him inquiringly. 'In my office,' he said, striding swiftly across the room, and her 'Miss Ashley? Hold on, will you? I have a call for you,' was terminated by the closing of his door.

'Isabel?' He practically snatched up the phone, grimacing at the sudden acceleration of his pulse. He was out of condition, he told himself fiercely, admitting no other reason for his laboured breathing. Sinking down on to the corner of his desk, he drew a steadying gulp of air. 'Isabel, this is Alex—Seton. My uncle asked me to get in touch with you.'

CHAPTER TWO

THE PHONE rang as Isabel was folding clothes into her suitcase. Jason, she thought immediately, unable to think of anyone else who might be ringing her at a quarter to five in the afternoon and, abandoning her packing, she went to answer it. Perhaps he was ringing to say the trip was off, she reflected hopefully, reaching for the receiver. A long weekend in Scotland at this particular point in her life was something she could have done without.

The girl's voice at the other end of the line was unfamiliar however. 'Miss Ashley?' she said. No one Jason employed would address her as 'Miss Ashley'. 'Hold on, will you? I have a call for you.'

Isabel moistened her lips. All of a sudden, she was back in the intimidating splendour of the lawyer's office, hearing the dry tones of Virginia Denby's solicitor telling her that she had inherited the old lady's shares in Denby Industries, and she instinctively knew that this call had something to do with that. Who else but Robert Seton would address her as *Miss* Ashley, losing no opportunity to underline his achievement in severing her connection with the Seton family?

She was tempted to ring off without speaking to the man. His company solicitors had already been in touch with her own, offering to buy back the shares at a substantially increased premium, and she had told them she was not interested. Evidently Robert Seton was not satisfied with her answer. She knew he would do anything in his power to prevent her from seeing Chris again. If he only knew . . .

19

'Isabel?'

Her hand trembled at the unwillingly familiar tones. She did not need his 'Isabel, this is Alex,' with 'Seton' added, almost as an afterthought, to identify her caller. Now she really wanted to slam down the receiver, and only the knowledge that Vinnie had expected more of her forced her to suffer his introduction.

'Alex,' she acknowledged flatly. And then, with irony, 'What a surprise!'

'Is it?' Unexpectedly, his voice was curt. 'Yes, well—Uncle Robert is out of the country at the moment, so he asked me to—stand in for him, so to speak.'

'Who better?' put in Isabel caustically, and his intake of breath proved her gibe had found its mark.

'Nevertheless,' he persisted, and she could tell it was an effort for him to control his temper, 'I wonder if it would be convenient for you to call in at my office tomorrow morning at—say——' She heard him flicking through the pages of his diary. 'Um—twelve-thirty?'

'I'm afraid not.' The Scottish trip was suddenly very attractive to her. 'I shall be out of town for the next few days. The earliest I could see you would be—oh——next Wednesday.'

His impatience was almost palpable. 'Next Wednesday,' he echoed through his teeth. 'I see.'

'It's the truth.' For some reason it was important that he should believe her. After all, the last thing she wanted was for him to think she was afraid to see him. Sooner or later, she would have to. She had accepted that when she accepted Vinnie's shares. 'I'm leaving for Perth first thing in the morning. I work for Jason Ferry now, and he's leased a castle over-looking Loch Tay for the weekend.' She crossed her fingers. 'It should be quite an exciting trip. I'm looking forward to it.'

'In May?' Alex was sceptical. 'I hope you get to keep your clothes on.'

Isabel's teeth dug into the soft skin of her lower lip. 'I always do,' she countered tautly. 'You should know that.'

'People change,' he retorted carelessly, and she knew an overwhelming desire to slap his lean, sardonic face. 'In any case,' he continued, 'I should have thought your unexpected windfall would have enabled you to give up an occupation you always professed to dislike.'

'Ah, but that was before I knew the Setons, Alex,' she declared maliciously. 'Compared to living with your family, photographic modelling is a breeze! And I wasn't working for Jason when I married Chris.' And let him make what he liked of that!

However, Alex let her remarks go without retaliation, and she wondered uneasily if she wasn't handling this badly. Surely she ought to be able to speak to him without resorting to insults. When she had first learned of Virginia Denby's generosity, she had determined to face her erstwhile in-laws with dignity and discretion. Yet, here she was, on the verge of kicking and clawing, like the ambitious bitch he had always thought her.

'Anyway,' she said now, adopting what she hoped was a conciliatory tone, 'I can't imagine why you should want us to meet. Any company business can surely be dealt with by my solicitors, and as you're not a member of the Denby board——'

'I've just told you,' Alex interrupted her smoothly. 'My uncle has asked me to deal with the situation in his absence, and as you were, nominally at least, a member of the family, a less—shall we say, formal transaction seems appropriate.'

Isabel's tawny brows drew together in some confusion. 'I'm afraid I—what particular transaction are you talking about?'

She heard him sigh. 'What transaction do you think I mean?' he enquired evenly.

'I don't know.' She frowned. 'Are there some papers I should have read and haven't?'

'Papers?' Alex snorted. 'Look, let's stop playing with words, shall we? I mean the shares, of course. Lady Denby's shares. You do remember them, don't you?'

Isabel's hand sought the cushioned back of her rocking-chair. Almost objectively, she admired the peach-coloured lacquer of her nails, that were such a subtle contrast to the dark green velvet of the cushion, but all the while her brain was racing with the turmoil of her thoughts.

'Are you still there?'

Her silence had initiated the question, and shaking her head in an effort to clear her reasoning, she said quietly, 'I thought I had made my position plain. Your grandmother left those shares to me. I—I intend to respect her wishes.'

There was a brief, but charged, pause, and then Alex said harshly, 'So why am I speaking with you now?'

Isabel swallowed. She could have asked him the same question. Indeed, if his uncle had asked him to contact her, it might be difficult for him to find a convincing answer. Or maybe it had been his idea. Just what was he playing at? Surely he didn't imagine he could trick her into handing the shares over. Her face burned at the thought that he might think he could succeed where his uncle had failed.

'Maybe you should ask yourself that,' she retorted now, refusing to be daunted by the prospect of his anger, but she could almost feel his antagonism.

'What is that supposed to mean?' he enquired, with

biting coldness, and throwing caution to the winds, she told him.

'You never could keep away from me, could you, Alex?' she taunted. 'That's what made you so mad. The fact that I had married Chris, when you were still available!'

She put the receiver down then, without waiting for his response. Whatever it was, whatever form his counter-attack might take, she had no wish to hear it, and she hoped that by the time she came back from Scotland, the whole thing would have blown over. It was obviously an attempt to get her to think again about the advisability of retaining the shares, and she wondered if, in spite of his oft-professed determination not to get involved in Denby business, Alex had finally accepted his heritage. After all, his mother had been a Denby, and he was too like his uncle to ignore the family trait.

Shaking her head, dismissing the faint feeling of unease that still lingered, Isabel walked back into the next room to continue her packing. The suitcase she intended to take with her was open on the bed, and she struggled to remember what she had put in and what she hadn't. The phone call had distracted her, and it was difficult to concentrate on a mundane chore like packing when her brain was still troubled by the things Alex had said. Nevertheless, she had to be ruthless and put all thoughts of the Seton family to the back of her mind, even if Alex's call had rekindled all her doubts about the legacy.

The suitcase wasn't full when she had completed her task, but although she and the other models would be away for five days, most of the time would be spent wearing the clothes sent by the agency. All she really needed was a couple of gowns suitable for evening wear, some casual gear and her toothbrush. Even her make-up would be put on by an expert, and her own selection of creams and eye make-up slotted easily into the canvas tote bag she carried.

Moving across to the mirrored vanity unit, Isabel made a half-hearted attempt to sort out the perfumes she intended to take with her. Her favourite, by Nina Ricci, she wore all the time, but for evenings she preferred something a little heavier. However, her attention was soon diverted by the image of her hands in the mirror, and resisting the urge to turn away, she let her gaze drift upward.

How long was it since any of the Setons had seen her, she wondered, running her fingertips along the line of her cheekbones. Three years? Four? Or was it longer? Certainly, it was all of four years since she had severed her connection with the family. Four years! It seemed a lifetime. So much had happened, and there had been so much she wanted to forget.

Smoky grey eyes encountered their reflection in the mirror, and she glimpsed a fleeting shadow in their depths. But the shadow was quickly banished, erased by a determination not to betray any emotion, even to herself, and instead she acknowledged their dark-lashed beauty. Her eyes had always been her best attribute and, together with features of reasonable attractiveness, had made her living, if not her fortune. Her nose was long, but at least it was straight, and high cheekbones could be a bane, particularly if she allowed herself to get too thin. After the divorce, her face had looked almost angular, and it had taken many months before the hollows filled out again. Her mouth was too wide, the upper lip too narrow, the lower lip too full. But it parted over teeth that were square and white and even, and Jason always said it had a sexy curve.

She grimaced now. Jason would say anything to get his own way, and lately he had revealed a totally unexpected possessiveness where she was concerned.

She hoped it wasn't going to become a problem. She liked Jason. She was grateful to him for giving her the chance to re-establish her career after her marriage failed. But she didn't love him. She didn't love anyone. Love was an emotion she couldn't afford. She had tried it once and it was far too destructive.

It was almost six and, deciding she deserved a cup of coffee, she walked back into the living-room and through it to the kitchen. The apartment was not large. In many ways it was small and inconvenient, in that all the rooms led out of one another, a fact which afforded little privacy when she had guests. But she lived alone, the place was hers, and mostly she didn't mind its shortcomings. It was the first real home she had known, and certainly it was the first home she had ever owned.

She had been brought up in a children's home. Her mother had abandoned her when she was only a few days old, and the somewhat ugly little girl she had become had not attracted would-be adoptive parents. She had always been tall for her age, and her long skinny limbs had contrasted unfavourably with those of smaller, chubbier children. In addition to which, red hair did not seem to find approval among the home's visitors, and the tight braids it was always confined in had accentuated her naturally pale skin. She had never looked strong, and the fact that she was as healthy as an ox had not convinced anyone. It wasn't until she was about fourteen, and her body began to fill out, that people's opinion started to change. The carroty hair had mellowed with age into a rich, dark red, the thin features had acquired a narrow-boned beauty, and the long, awkward limbs had become shapely and elegant. The ugly duckling had turned into a swan, and the trustees at the children's home didn't quite know what to do with her.

She supposed it was natural that she should turn to modelling as a career. In that respect she had been lucky, for one of the governors of the home had had connections with one of the larger model agencies in the city, and by the time she was twenty, she was fairly well established in commercial advertising. And then, she had met Chris, they had got married, and in her innocence, she had imagined they would live happily ever after. How wrong she had been . . .

The sound of her doorbell interrupted her thoughts. Strangely enough, it was not the intercom from downstairs, that visitors usually used to gain access to the building. It was the bell attached to her front door. And although she realised her caller could be one of her fellow tenants, she had purposely kept aloof from the occupants of the other apartments. It wasn't that she was unfriendly. But her privacy was important to her. That was why a troubled expression entered her eyes as she heard the bell peal again.

She wasn't prepared for visitors, she fretted, glancing down at the sloppy yellow track suit she had worn home from the gym. Her feet were bare, her face was devoid of any make-up, and the tangled mass of her hair would need a thorough brushing to tame it. She had intended to do her packing, give herself a facial, enjoy a long luxurious soak in the bath, and then eat a snack supper as she watched the late film. Who could possibly expect to thwart her plans? She could only think of Jason, and her lips compressed impatiently as she walked towards the door.

Even so, it paid to be cautious and, attaching the chain, she called, 'Who is it?' before releasing the latch.

There was a moment's silence, during which time she wondered if her caller had given up and gone away. But if it was Jason, she knew better than to believe that this was so, and waiting for his answer, she expelled a heavy sigh.

'Isabel?' said a voice at last, and although it was male, it was definitely not Jason's. He did not have that distinctive timbre to his tones, nor did his voice send a wave of shocked resentment sweeping over her. 'Open the door! We didn't finish our conversation.'

Isabel swallowed, turning to press her shoulders against the panels. Alex! Here! She couldn't believe it.

'Isabel!'

The edge to his voice was unmistakable, and she thought how typical it was of all the Setons, that they should believe she would jump to their tune. Did Alex really believe that by side-stepping the building's security system, he could barge in here, uninvited? He was totally intractable, and too arrogant to be true.

'Isabel! I know you're there. Don't you have the guts to open the door? Or does hanging up on someone constitute the whole gamut of your resolution?'

Isabel's jaw clenched. This was ridiculous. She was standing here, cringing, and letting the man she despised most in the world threaten her from the other side of a door. He was wrong. She did have guts. And if she hadn't rushed to speak to him, it wasn't because she was scared to do so.

Turning, she hurriedly lifted the latch, and knew a sense of irritation when she fumbled with it. She didn't want him to think he had disconcerted her, though she still kept the safety chain in place.

The door opened to the width of the chain, and steeling herself, she faced the man outside for the first time since her divorce from his cousin. 'Well, Alex! How nice,' she greeted him tauntingly. 'I didn't know you stooped to breaking and entering. But then, nothing the Setons did would ever really surprise me.'

Alex propped his shoulder against the door. 'I don't propose to stand here all night, Isabel,' he said, almost pleasantly. 'Either you open the door properly and let me in, or I break it. It's up to you. Make up your mind.'

Isabel's tongue circled her lips. 'You wouldn't dare.'

'Wouldn't I? Try me. And I'd hazard a guess that you'd have more to lose than I would. Your neighbours wouldn't like it. They might even call the police. Think how embarrassing that would be in a conservative building like this.'

'You bastard!'

'That's more like the Isabel I remember.' He straightened up. 'Open the door.'

Isabel slammed it shut, but only to dislodge the chain and secure the catch. 'It's open,' she muttered, backing away into the living-room, and then turned her back on him as he came into the flat.

He hadn't changed, she thought bitterly. She might have gone through a personal trauma, but Alex Seton looked just as enigmatic as ever. She didn't even have to look at him to recall the dark, almost black, eyes, set between thick, stubby lashes, in a face that was too hard to be called handsome. He was the only man whose height had topped hers by some four inches, and whose lean muscular body owed its fitness to a high metabolism, rather than to a grim devotion to athleticism. So far as she remembered, he had always avoided sports, though he used to swim regularly at a health club in London. He was rich and successful, and immensely attractive to women. But he was also ruthless, as Isabel had learned to her cost.

He came into the living-room of the apartment now, his hands pushed carelessly into the pockets of his jacket. His suit was dark blue, and expensive, she surmised and, like all the clothes she had seen him wear, it fitted his lithe frame with loving indulgence. As he moved, the width of his shoulders was clearly outlined beneath the fine fabric, while the narrow cut of the trousers exposed the powerful muscles of his thighs. She didn't want to look at him, but she couldn't avoid it, particularly as any show of reticence was likely to work to his advantage, not hers.

Alex, meanwhile, was looking intently about the room, and she wondered what he thought of her modest domain. Certainly it could be nothing like the apartments he was used to, and compared to the spacious elegance of Nazeby it must appear cluttered and restricted. After all, much of the furniture had come from the saleroom, the actual purchase price of the flat straining her resources to the limit.

'What do you want?' she demanded now, deciding it was safer to take the initiative than wait for him to do so, and he turned his appraising gaze in her direction.

'You don't change, do you, Isabel?' he remarked obliquely, and she knew an angry sense of frustration. 'I don't think you've ever felt anything deeply in your whole life. That's what makes it so unbelievable that Vinnie should have been taken in by you.'

Isabel drew a breath. 'Is that why you've come here? To talk about your grandmother?' She shrugged. 'She was a dear old lady, and I loved her very much. What more is there to say?'

'Loved?' Alex's thin-lipped mouth curled. 'Oh, spare me that, please! You've never loved anyone, but yourself. Not Chris, not my uncle——'

'You're wrong. I did love Vinnie,' broke in Isabel indignantly, and then, realising that once again she was letting him put her on the defensive, she forced a mocking smile. 'What's the matter, Alex?' she countered lazily. 'Are you jealous?'

The faint trace of colour that entered his narrow face at her words was worth the effort. So, she thought ruefully, that was the only way to deal with him. More difficult, perhaps, but oh, so rewarding!

'As I said, you don't change,' he retorted, spearing her with a crippling gaze. 'Beautiful, but immoral. And selfish to the core. Thank God, Chris had the sense to walk away from you. He may not have found anyone else yet, but at least he's happy.'

Isabel stiffened, but she refused to let him see his words could still hurt her. After all, she had heard them before. She ought to be used by now to that particular offensive. But it was some time since she had come under attack, and she hadn't yet marshalled her defences.

'Anyway, I didn't come here to get involved in old hostilities,' Alex went on presently, and Isabel shrugged.

'To create new ones instead?' she suggested provokingly, and had the temporary satisfaction of another minor victory.

'To talk about your change of heart,' he corrected her grimly. 'Although, as you don't appear to have a heart, perhaps that was an unfortunate choice of phrase. Your change of—mind, shall we say? The reasons behind your communicating with my uncle, which seem at variance with your present attitude.'

Isabel blinked. 'I beg your pardon?'

Alex gave her a weary look. 'Let's cut the chaff, shall we? Just tell me what you want, and I'll try to accommodate you. Uncle Robert will pay whatever it takes to get those shares back. Name your own price. You have the advantage.'

Isabel stared at him. 'Would you believe me if I told you I didn't know what the hell you were talking about?'

'No.' Alex rocked back on to his heels and then forward on to the balls of his feet. 'Isabel, there only is one subject on which we can still communicate. Don't play me for a fool. You know what I'm talking about.'

Isabel shook her head. 'All right. I accept that you've come here to try and persuade me to sell the shares, but I don't see where your uncle comes in. Any communication I've had with him has always been through my solicitors.'

'Has it?' Alex absorbed this in silence for a moment. And then he pulled one hand out of his pocket and pushed long brown fingers into the thick dark hair at his nape. 'So, Uncle Robert didn't tell me that, but no matter. Evidently, your solicitors intimated your desire to discuss it further. As I say, tell me what you want. I'll speak to my uncle and get back to you tomorrow—or next week, if you are going away for the weekend.'

'*If* I am?' Isabel controlled her resentment with an effort. 'Look, I'm sorry, Alex, but I still don't know anything about this.'

'You're lying.'

'No, I'm not!' She was incensed by his intransigence. 'I think you'd better go back to your uncle and find out exactly what he's playing at. I didn't contact him. My solicitors didn't contact him. And what's more, I don't believe your story any more than you do mine.'

Alex stared at her angrily now. 'You're saying you've never thought about selling the shares?'

Isabel nodded. 'Yes.'

'Then why would my——?'

Alex broke off in the middle of his question, and she saw the flash of illumination that crossed his face. As if a veil had lifted, she glimpsed the sudden comprehension in his expression, but then the mask descended, and she could no longer guess his thoughts.

'I think I'd better go,' he said abruptly, pulling his other hand out of his pocket and fastening a single button on his jacket. 'It seems I was mistaken. I've evidently misunderstood my uncle's message. He must have hoped you'd come to your senses. Vinnie may

have left you the shares, but she never expected you
to keep them.'

'What you mean is, your uncle hoped you'd have
more success than he did,' exclaimed Isabel contemptuously, disgusted by the realisation that Alex would
support his uncle, whatever the circumstances. For a
moment, just for a moment, she had thought she had
seen disillusionment in his face, and she had actually
felt sympathy for him. But whatever she had seen, it
was firmly controlled now, and it was galling to hear
him defend a man who was totally unscrupulous.

'I have no intention of debating my uncle's intentions with you,' Alex stated, walking towards the door
and, watching him, Isabel wondered if he was really
as indifferent as he seemed. In his place, she would
have been as mad as hell, but Alex, as always, revealed
none of his feelings.

'You've had a wasted journey then,' she ventured
softly, curiously unwilling to let it lie. 'Uncle Robert
must be laughing up his sleeve at the prospect of you
and me being at cross purposes. I mean, he couldn't
actually have hoped that you would influence me.
Doesn't he know that you hate my guts?'

Alex's expression hardened. 'You put it too strongly,
Isabel,' he retorted, pausing in the act of reaching for
the Yale lock. 'To hate someone, one must first have
feelings towards them. Thankfully, that was not the
case so far as I was concerned. I admired you, as one
does any unusual object. But I didn't desire you,
Isabel. That's where you made your mistake.'

Isabel caught her breath. 'That's not true.'

'I'm afraid it is.' With a jerk, he had the door open,
and had stepped outside. 'Keep your shares, Isabel.
Take them to bed with you. As you judge everyone in
terms of their bank balance, you should find them
very reassuring.'

The door slammed on her angry retort, and although

she longed to charge after him and rake her nails across his smug, complacent face, she didn't. Instead, she dropped the latch, slid the bolt and put the chain back into position, as if by shutting out his material presence she could eliminate him from her thoughts. But, of course, she couldn't. Apart from anything else, the faint aroma of some tangy soap or shaving lotion he used still lingered in the apartment, and even though she opened the windows she could still smell it when she went to bed.

CHAPTER THREE

'YOUR cousin is here to see you, Alex . Shall I send him in?'

Diana Laurence's enquiry was voiced from the intercom at his elbow, and Alex gave an impatient sigh. 'Why?'

'Why is he here, or why send him in?' queried Diana drily, and, as her boss revealed his irritation, 'I don't know. Do you want me to ask him?'

Alex hesitated. 'What time is my next appointment?'

'You don't have one.'

'I do now.' Alex's response was clipped. 'Give us—oh, fifteen minutes, and then break it up, hmm?'

'If you say so.' Diana sounded reluctant. 'So—shall I send him in? He can hear this conversation, you know.'

'Only your side of it,' declared Alex curtly. 'OK, Diana. If you must. But don't forget; fifteen minutes only.'

Alex was putting aside the file he had been studying when his cousin, Christopher, entered his office. Sliding the calculator he had been using into a drawer, he rose to meet the man who had once been Isabel Ashley's husband, and he was annoyed by the realisation that he should think of Chris in that way.

'Sit down,' he said, after their initial greeting. 'To what do I owe the pleasure; or is this a social call?'

Christopher Seton laughed and lounged into the chair opposite. Crossing his legs, he rested his hands loosely on his knees. Like his cousin, he was wearing a three-piece suit, but whereas Alex's choice was dark

34

and conservative, Christopher's outfit was much more flamboyant. He was wearing a cream tweed jacket with a matching waistcoat and pants, and instead of a tie, a cream and yellow cravat filled the neck of his shirt. They were clothes more suited to the race-track than the office, and Alex guessed this visit had been an afterthought. He and Chris seldom saw one another these days. It wasn't that he avoided his cousin; if they met at Nazeby, they were always civil to one another. But since they had both become adults, they had found they had nothing in common, and the affair of Isabel had only served to widen the breach.

'How are you, Alex?' Chris asked now, and his cousin knew a sense of irritation out of all proportion to the inconvenience Chris's arrival had created.

However, he hid his feelings admirably, as he responded, 'I'm fine. How about you?'

'Fine, fine.' Chris's lips twitched. 'Losing more than I'm winning, but what's new? It helps to pass the time. You should try it.'

Alex's expression was controlled. 'Not my scene, Chris. You should know that. I prefer a surer way of earning a living.'

'Oh, yes.' Chris's fuller features took on a familiar expression. 'Good old Alex! The example to us all. Well, you ought to lighten up, old man, or Dad will mould you in his image. You know you're his favourite. I never stood a chance.'

Alex sighed. 'That's not true, Chris.'

'Isn't it?' His cousin regarded him shrewdly. 'You wouldn't say that if you could see him. This business over Isabel is tearing him apart.'

'So that's it.' With an exclamation of disgust, Alex pushed back his chair and got abruptly to his feet. 'Your father sent you here, didn't he? To try and justify what he did. You don't really believe I'm your father's favourite. That was just a ruse to try and get my sympathy.'

Chris expelled his breath on a weary sigh. 'Would I do that?'

'If he made it worth your while, yes.' Alex had no illusions about his cousin.

'That's not fair!'

Alex regarded him resignedly for a moment, then he shook his head. 'What did he say?'

'Who? Dad?'

'Who else?'

Chris flicked an imaginary speck of dust from his cuff, and then said carefully, 'He's very upset, Alex. You hurt his feelings. He's not used to anyone treating him like that.'

'Tough.'

'And over Isabel, too!' Chris looked up at him incredulously. 'I mean, if there was any way we could get those shares back again, we should try it. I don't know what Vinnie was thinking of to do such a thing. They were my shares, Alex; mine! How could she leave them to her?'

Alex's lips tightened. 'As a consolation, perhaps?' he remarked sardonically, and Chris was considering his words when he looked up and caught his expression.

'Oh, very funny,' he muttered, realising Alex was being sarcastic. 'Well, anyway, I think you're behaving very badly. Dad was only thinking of the company, you know. And you'll expect a share of that, as well as me.'

'I don't expect anything,' retorted Alex flatly. 'Denby Industries is all yours. Now, if that's all you came to say, I do have work to do——'

'What's she like?'

Chris's unexpected intervention caught Alex unawares, and he felt the warmth invade his neck around his collar. 'I beg your pardon?' he said, though he knew perfectly well what Chris had said, and his cousin moistened full red lips before repeating his enquiry. 'Isabel. Has she changed much?'

Alex considered his answer. 'I—not a lot,' he admitted reluctantly. 'She's older, of course, but aren't we all?'

Chris leant forward. 'Is she—is she still as beautiful?'

'If you like that sort of thing.' Alex took a deep breath. 'Look, what is this, Chris? Why do you care what she looks like?'

'I don't. At least, not really.' Chris lay back in his chair again, and Alex's fingers itched to pull him out of it and eject him from his office. 'But you have to admit, I had good taste. I used to get quite a kick out of taking her places. People used to look at her, you know. Men, especially. They used to envy me.' He shook his head. 'What a pity!'

Alex kept his temper with difficulty. 'Chris,' he said warningly and, with a gesture of compliance, the younger man got to his feet.

'All right, all right, I'm going,' he exclaimed defensively. 'Can't a fellow reminisce from time to time? I wasn't to know she'd turn out to be a super-bitch, was I? Thank heavens you weren't attracted to her. It was bad enough finding out she was cheating on me. Imagine how I'd have felt if you'd been involved.'

Alex's mouth compressed. 'She's not my type.'

Chris snorted. 'Oh, thanks. That's some consolation, I suppose.'

'You know what I mean.'

Chris got to his feet. He wasn't as tall as his cousin, and he looked at him now from beneath lowered lids. 'I suppose I do,' he conceded. Then, 'But what about this business over Dad? Are you going to let that cow ruin your relationship?'

Alex groaned. 'Chris——'

'Well, as you guessed, it's why I came. The old man's like a bear with a sore head these days. What with Isabel's solicitors refusing to discuss any sale, and you treating him like a leper! Can't you see his motives were honourable, even if the way he went about it wasn't? Go see him, Alex. Make your peace.'

Penny Hollister seconded Chris's request later that day. Penny, who was a stewardess with Middle European Airlines, had arrived back from Kuwait the day before, but Alex had had a dinner engagement that night, and they had been unable to get together until this evening. Now, as they shared a bottle of wine at the small Italian restaurant near Alex's house in Knightsbridge, he had been forced to admit they would not be spending the weekend at Nazeby that he had previously suggested. He had glossed over the more personal details of his encounter with his cousin's ex-wife, but he had had to tell Penny why he had gone to see her.

'Well, I think your grandmother must have been a little dotty, whatever her doctors say,' Penny declared now, her disappointment at being denied her trip to Nazeby colouring her tones. 'What was she trying to prove? I mean, they were divorced, weren't they, your cousin and this woman? Why should she make her a beneficiary when she's no longer a member of the family?'

Alex was non-committal. He didn't like to hear his grandmother described as mildly demented, no matter how upset Penny might be feeling, and he was glad when their bolognese was served, and he could concentrate on that.

'What's she like, anyway?' Penny asked, winding a long string of spaghetti round her fork, and Alex watched her for several seconds before saying dismissingly, 'She's a woman.'

'I know that.' Penny grimaced in mock-reproval. 'But what does she look like? Is she good-looking? She must have something to have attracted your cousin.'

Alex didn't really want to discuss it, but he realised any reluctance on his part could be construed as prejudice. And the last thing he wanted Penny to think was that he had any personal reason to deny her request.

'Um—well, she's a bit like you,' he replied at last, and as he did so, he realised how true that was. The two girls were alike, although if he was honest, he would have to admit that Penny was only a pale reflection of her *alter ego*. Isabel's hair was richly coloured; Penny's was amber; Isabel's eyes were a greenish grey; Penny's irises were hazel; Isabel's mouth was wide and provocative; Penny's lips were unremarkable . . .

'Like me?' Penny said, looking at him archly. 'How intriguing! Tell me more.'

'There's nothing more to tell.' Except that Isabel was taller, and slimmer; and he resented the suggestion that he had made any connection.

'You don't like her, do you?' Penny ventured now, sliding her hand across the table and caressing his wrist. She had sensed his irritation, and she was eager to restore his humour. 'If it makes you angry, we won't talk about it any more. But do you think she's worth the sacrifice of being at odds with your uncle?'

Alex's nostrils flared. 'I don't think the two things are mutually compatible. My opinion of Isabel has nothing to do with my argument with my uncle. Let's leave it at that, shall we? I dare say Uncle Robert and I will sort out our differences eventually.'

'But not before this weekend,' bemoaned Penny

ruefully. 'Damn Isabel Ashley! And damn your grandmother, too.'

Alex made no comment. He was grateful for the opportunity to change the subject, and for a while their conversation turned to less controversial matters. But then, after the meal, when they were waiting for a liqueur to round off the evening. Penny suddenly said, 'What does she do?' and Alex's feeling of tranquillity fled.

'What does who do?' he asked. But he knew. It was as if the subject fascinated Penny. Hearing that they looked alike had evidently aroused her interest, and although she knew he wouldn't like it, she had to take the chance.

'Isabel Ashley,' she said at once, giving him a pleading look. 'Don't be mad. I'm curious, that's all. Maybe she doesn't work for her living. I just wondered if she did.'

'She's a photographic model,' said Alex flatly. 'She does layouts for catalogues and things, and occasionally she appears in TV commercials. Does that satisfy you?'

Penny's eyes widened. 'Would I know her face if I saw it?'

'I doubt it.' Alex was impatient. 'She's no Marie Helvin. There are dozens of girls, just like her. Few of them ever make it big.'

'I suppose not.' Penny was thoughtful. 'All the same . . . ' She shrugged. 'She did meet your cousin.'

'Yes, she did that,' agreed Alex sardonically, and when his brandy came, he swallowed it in two gulps. 'Right. Shall we go? Before I begin to wonder if Chris is the reason you so desperately wanted to spend the weekend at Nazeby.'

'As if that was a possibility!' Penny exclaimed later, hugging his arm as they walked the short distance to where Alex had left his car. 'I have met him, you know. He came to your apartment that Sunday, wanting to borrow some cash because all the banks were closed.' She grimaced. 'He's not my type at all. He has such a weak face, don't you think?'

Alex regarded her tolerantly as he unlocked the Ferrari. 'Well, that's my grandmother and my cousin you've insulted. Anyone else?'

Penny coloured. 'I'm sorry. I just didn't want you to even think I was interested in Chris. No, I was just curious about his ex-wife, that's all. I don't believe you ever told me why they split up.'

'Some other time,' said Alex briefly, swinging open his door. 'I've got some work to do after I've taken you home.'

Penny's face dropped. 'You're not coming in?'

'Not tonight,' said Alex, reaching for the ignition. 'I've got to have a report ready for tomorrow morning, and right now, it's only half written.'

Penny gave him a sulky look. 'You should have said. I could have easily got a Chinese take-away, and washed my hair instead.'

Alex glanced her way. 'Who's complaining?'

'I am.' She hunched her shoulders. 'First of all, our weekend's been blown out of the water by this silly disagreement you've had with your uncle, and now you don't have time to go to bed with me because you've got some stupid report to write! What did you expect?'

'All right, all right. We'll go to bed together then,' said Alex expressionlessly. 'But I shall have to leave straight after——'

'No, you won't!'

'The report won't write itself.'

'That's not what I meant.' She sniffed. 'If you think I'd just let you *use* me——'

'I understood we used each other,' Alex overrode her coldly. 'I thought we agreed our work would

always come first. I don't object when you fly off to
Cairo or Bahrain, or some European capital at a
moment's notice. Why should you complain when I
tell you I have commitments, too?'

'Because I've just come back from the Middle East,'
she exclaimed indignantly. 'We haven't been together
for over a week! I need you, Alex.'

'I'm sorry.'

'No, you're not.' She flung herself away from him.
'And I can't help wondering why it isn't the same for
you as it is for me. How do I know what you get up
to while I'm out of the country? You could have
another woman. I'd never get to know.'

Alex expelled a heavy breath. 'This is ridiculous!'

'Is it? Is it?' Penny slumped in the seat. 'I wish I
could believe you.'

Alex slowed to accommodate a pedestrian crossing.
'Does it matter?' he queried wearily. 'I don't put any
conditions on you.'

'No, you don't, do you?' she countered bitterly. 'So
what am I supposed to glean from that? Is there
someone else?'

Alex's face was set. 'I don't think that's part of our
agreement.'

'So there is,' she cried tearfully.

'I didn't say that.' Alex swung the car into the
forecourt of the apartment block where Penny lived,
and brought the car to a standstill. 'But would you
believe that I was telling you the truth if I denied it?'

Penny gulped. 'If—if we could trust one
another——'

'Trust is for kids, Penny. And for those rare beings
who find a lasting relationship. It's not for us. We
each professed to want our independence.'

Penny's lip quivered. 'And if I've changed my mind?'

'I haven't,' said Alex callously and, getting out of
the car, he walked round to open her door for her.

'Good night, Penny. Sleep well.'

He was getting into the car again when she seemed to come to her senses. 'When will I see you again?'

'I'll give you a ring,' he promised glibly, and then, before she could put any further restraints upon him, he set the wheels in motion with a spinning of the tyres.

Kerry was still up when he got back to Eaton Mews and his bushy brows arched enquiringly when his employer walked in.

'Sure, and you're an early bird,' he exclaimed, switching off his television and following Alex into the kitchen. 'Now what can I get you? Some coffee? A cup of tea? Or would you rather have something stronger? There's that bottle of fire-water your uncle brought you back from Brazil.'

'Coke will do,' Alex assured him flatly, extracting a can from the door of the fridge. 'And I don't want anything to eat either. I've just had dinner, and I've got some work to do.'

'Ah.'

Kerry nodded, and Alex drank half the can before wiping his mouth on the back of his hand and regarding the smaller man dourly. 'Ah what?' he demanded.

Kerry shifted a little awkwardly now. 'Ah—that's why you're back so soon,' he volunteered defensively. 'Because you've got some work to do. I assumed you'd be spending——'

'You should never assume anything, Kerry,' said Alex, brushing past him on the way to his study. Shrugging off his jacket with one arm, he drained the can with the other. 'I don't want to be disturbed, understand? I'll see you in the morning.'

'Yes, sir.'

Kerry watched his employer disappear through the door that led into his private sanctum and pulled a wry face. If he was any judge, it wasn't just the weight of work that was bugging the man tonight. Mr Seton had something else on his mind, or he was a lepre- chaun's uncle!

In all honesty, Alex was admitting much the same thing to himself. Flinging himself into the chair at his desk, he acknowledged that the excuse he had given Penny wouldn't quite hold water. Oh, he had a report to write, but there was no specific urgency for it. He had actually told his client it might take several days to compile, and he had only used that as an excuse to get out of an unwelcome situation. But why? Why hadn't he wanted to go to bed with Penny tonight, when for the past six months they had had a more than satisfactory relationship?

One solution to his dilemma was totally unaccept- able to him. The idea that his recent encounter with Isabel Ashley should in some way have influenced his decision tonight was almost laughable, only he wasn't entertained. Apprehensive, perhaps; angry, certainly; but not in any way amused.

Pulling his tie away from his collar, he tore the knot free and tossed it impatiently across his desk. For once, the elegantly appointed room gave him no pleasure, and the lamplight glinting over polished mahogany and Moroccan leather was just a means of illuminating his unease. He didn't feel like working. He didn't feel like doing anything. But he was sensible enough to realise where too much introspection might lead and, gritting his teeth, he reached for the pile of documents arranged neatly in a metal tray. He had always been able to find peace of mind in his work, and when Kerry risked poking his head round the door before going to bed, he found his employer firmly engrossed in a complicated financial analysis.

Robert Seton rang Alex the next morning.

'Do you want to speak to him?' asked Diana, mindful of her employer's mood the previous day after his cousin had departed. 'You have an appointment at eleven.'

Alex hesitated. Then, 'Why not?' he conceded, after a moment. 'OK, Diana. Put him through.'

His uncle was evidently delighted at his success. 'Does this mean you've forgiven me, Alex?' he exclaimed, causing the younger man no small feeling of self-derision. 'Chris told me that he's spoken to you. I don't usually approve of his interference, as you know, but in this instance, I'm inclined to reserve judgement.'

Alex caught his lower lip between his teeth for a moment before replying. He was not unaware that his decision to speak to his uncle was due in no small measure to the restless night he had just spent, rather than to any persuasion his cousin had exerted. But why shouldn't Chris take the credit? he mused wearily. He had no intention of telling Robert that Isabel Ashley had disturbed his sleep.

'What do you want, Uncle?' he inquired now, leaning back in his chair and resting the ankle of one leg across the knee of the other. 'I have an appointment in exactly four minutes. I'm not being rude, but I really don't have a lot of time.'

'I know what a busy man you are.' Robert Seton was conciliatory. 'And what I have to say won't take more than a couple of minutes. I just wanted to tell you that I'm still expecting you at Nazeby this weekend. And your charming friend of course. Chris is looking forward to seeing her again. He tells me she's a lovely girl.'

Alex sighed. 'I'm afraid I won't be able to make it this weekend after all, Uncle. Something has—come up. I'm sorry.'

Robert sighed, too. 'So you haven't forgiven me.'

'My decision has nothing to do with the affair over Isabel,' declared Alex shortly. 'It's simply that——'

'How can I believe you?' His uncle sounded desperate. 'Alex, the last time we met, face to face, you said some pretty scathing things about me, and about my business methods. All right. Maybe I did behave badly. Maybe I did send you to see that woman with some crazy idea that you might succeed where I failed. She always had a soft spot for you, you know that. Was it so unscrupulous to try and exploit the fact?'

'Yes.' Alex was adamant.

'Well—so be it. If you say so. But we're *family*, Alex. We can't allow that woman to be the cause of any more unpleasantness between us. Please, say you'll forget what I did. I really do want to see you.'

'Why?'

Robert gasped. 'Why do you think?'

Alex considered. 'The board meeting next week, perhaps.'

There was a pause, and the silence that ensued was heavy with frustration. A home run, reflected Alex shrewdly. Robert must be more distraught than he thought. He had evidently overlooked the fact that, as financial consultant to the company, his nephew received regular bulletins about all company matters. He already knew there was a meeting on Thursday.

'So,' Robert's voice was flat now, 'I could invite you in your business capacity.'

'In business hours.' Alex conceded the point.

'Oh, come on.' There was an edge to his uncle's voice. 'Not all your dealings are conducted in business hours. Can't you spare me one weekend? I really do need to talk to you.'

Alex paused. 'What about?'

'I thought you said you had a client pending.'

'I do.'

Robert grunted. 'Well, this may take longer than a few minutes. Have dinner with me this evening. We can talk about it then.'

'I'm afraid I have a dinner engagement,' said Alex flatly. 'If you could come here tomorrow——'

'Lunch, then,' said his uncle harshly. 'Or are you booked for lunch, too? What are you trying to do to me, Alex? Don't you think you owe me a few minutes of your time?'

Alex could have said he couldn't make it, but the affection he had always had for his uncle won out. At half-past twelve, he walked through the doors of the select Soho restaurant Robert had suggested, and joined his waiting relative in the adjacent bar.

'Gin and tonic?' enquired the older man, indicating his own glass, but Alex shook his head.

'Perrier water,' he insisted, sliding on to the stool beside him. 'I've got a heavy afternoon ahead of me.'

Robert grimaced, but he gave the bartender the order and then surveyed his nephew with unconcealed relief. 'I can't tell you how pleased I am to see you, Alex. And to know that we've ironed out our differences, too. We have ironed them out, haven't we?' he probed, when the younger man arched a sardonic eyebrow, and after a moment Alex inclined his head.

'I guess so,' he conceded drily, accepting the glass of iced Perrier water from the barman. 'So long as you're not about to ask me to undertake any more of your dirty work.'

Robert's mouth compressed. 'It wasn't like that, Alex. You know why I did it. Isabel—if she was going to listen to anyone, it had to be you.'

'But I had already refused that assignment,' Alex reminded him tersely, still feeling the tug of frustration in his stomach when he remembered how Robert had tricked him. 'Look, as far as Isabel Ashley is concerned, you're just going to have to live with it.'

'I can't.' Robert brought his balled fist down on the bar in silent protest. 'You don't realise what that woman's trying to do to me.'

Alex contained his impatience with an effort, looking away from his uncle to survey the discreetly lit restaurant that was visible beyond the curtained entrance to the bar. He should have known better than to believe Robert was prepared to let the situation ride. It was eating him up. That much was evident from the agitated way he kept toying with his glass, and the air of tension about him was not just a reaction to this meeting. He needed Alex, but mostly he needed someone to confide in.

Bringing his gaze back to his glass, Alex lifted it to swirl the ice around in the faintly sparkling mineral water. 'So,' he said, submitting to an unwilling stir of conscience, 'tell me. What is she doing?'

'Do you really want to know? You're not just humouring me?'

'I'm asking, aren't I?' Alex hid his resignation.

'All right.' Robert drew a steadying breath. 'All right, I'll tell you. She's blocking Denby's bid for Mattley Pharmaceuticals.'

Alex frowned now. 'Blocking your bid?' he echoed. 'How can she do that?'

'Don't you believe me?'

Robert was aggressive and, realising he was being presumptuous, Alex urged his uncle to go on.

'It's quite easy, really. She's voting her shares against mine. I've had prior notification from her solicitors, before the board meeting next week.'

Alex was confused. 'But Vinnie's shares only amounted to—what? Fifteen per cent, wasn't it?'

Robert groaned. 'I let her have your Aunt Ellen's shares when she died,' he admitted painfully. 'Vinnie had lost both her daughters, and I thought that by giving her Ellen's shares, it would help to keep one of them alive. I always assumed that when Vinnie died, they'd come back into the family.' He shook his head. 'And this is how she repays me!'

Alex stared at him. 'So that was why——'

'—why I was so shattered when the will was read?' Robert's lips twisted. 'Yes. It was quite a blow.'

'And you need a seventy-five per cent majority to push through the Mattley deal.'

'You've got it.'

Alex hesitated. 'So how many shares does Isabel —own?'

'Thirty per cent,' said his uncle flatly.

'*Thirty!*' Alex was stunned.

'Yes.' Robert shrugged. 'It's my fault, of course. If I hadn't been so stupidly sentimental, I wouldn't be in this position now. That's why I need your help, Alex. I don't expect you to get actively involved again, but perhaps you can give me some advice.'

CHAPTER FOUR

IT WAS after one o'clock when Isabel hurried into the restaurant. She had spent the morning at the hairdressers, having the ends of her hair trimmed, and a thorough conditioning had done much to tame its unruly wildness into a manageable state. Now, it was caught up on top of her head in a loose knot, with delicious tendrils of dark red silk nudging the collar of her dark blue jacket. Underneath the jacket, a purple suede button-through dress hugged the shapely contours of her thighs, and even without the heels that added inches to her height, she would have attracted attention.

Not that Isabel enjoyed her notoriety. She was indifferent to the fact that her entrance had caused a minor stir. Her years as a model had enabled her to acquire an immunity to inquisitive eyes, and right now her mind was focused on the fact that Jason had been waiting for over half an hour.

'I know,' she murmured unhappily, responding to his censure, as he rose to hold her chair for her. 'I'm late. But it wasn't my fault.'

Jason Ferry resumed his seat and regarded her sombrely. 'So whose fault was it, then?' he enquired coldly. 'Don't tell me you've just left the salon.'

'But I have,' protested Isabel anxiously. 'You know what it's like trying to get a taxi at this time of day. And then, when I did manage to get one, we got stuck in Charing Cross Road.'

'You should have phoned,' said Jason unreasonably, summoning the waiter. 'Two glasses of white wine, Claud. One with ice.'

Isabel sank back in her chair, slipping off her jacket as Jason gave the order. It no longer annoyed her that Jason hadn't asked her what she wanted before ordering. She was used to his high-handedness now, and besides, today she was relieved that he had not caused a scene. He was a strange man, in some ways. Childishly temperamental at times, and at others, infinitely kind and understanding. He was a conscientious worker, tireless in his pursuit of success for his models. Yet, at the same time, he could be sulky and impatient, taking offence at the slightest thing, and venting his spleen on those who were nearest to him.

She supposed he was a handsome man, although she had never been attracted by his fair good looks and stocky frame. Apart from the fact she wasn't interested in men, he reminded her too much of her ex-husband. And that was why she hoped his present proprietorial attitude towards her was not going to create problems.

'Well, at least the appointment was a success,' he remarked now, capturing her hand on the pretext of examining her nails. His thumb rubbed over the mauve lacquer the manicurist had applied before he brought her fingers to his lips. 'I'm sorry if I was rude. But I was getting quite worried about you.'

Isabel offered a smile, but she withdrew her hand from his grasp. 'No problem,' she said, picking up the glass the waiter had just set beside her and, avoiding Jason's possessive gaze, she looked round the room—straight into the eyes of Alex Seton.

To say she was surprised would have been an understatement. She was shocked, stunned, and not a little resentful that he should be there. After all, she had never seen him here before, and the thought immediately occurred to her that his presence was

intentional. But why? What did he have to gain? After
their recent encounter, it was the last thing she would
have expected. But then she saw his companion, and
the doubts she had been feeling crystallised.

Unknown to her, a little of the colour left her
cheeks at this discovery, and although she quickly
looked away, she could not hide her dismay from
Jason. The make-up the beautician had employed with
such effect earlier in the day only accentuated her
sudden pallor, and his brows drew together when he
noticed her expression.

'What is it?' he exclaimed, at once concerned on her
behalf. 'Is something wrong? Aren't you feeling well?
You can tell me.'

'It's nothing.' Isabel had no wish to draw Jason's
attention to the Setons. 'I—I just felt a bit faint, that's
all. I'm probably hungry. What shall we eat?'

Jason frowned. 'Are you sure you're telling me the
truth?'

Isabel gathered her defences and levelled a cool gaze
in his direction. 'I'm not in the habit of lying,' she
declared, lifting her glass to her lips. But although she
performed quite convincingly to Jason's wary eye, she
was intensely conscious of another, hostile, scrutiny.

'Very well.' Jason was obliged to believe her. He
picked up the menu the waiter had left lying by his
plate, and gave it a swift appraisal. 'What would you
like to eat?'

'Hello, Isabel.'

The much-hated, yet undeniably attractive, voice
relieved her of an immediate decision. Instead, as
Jason's features mirrored a taut reflection of his feelings at this interruption, she was obliged to
acknowledge the man who had paused beside their
table.

'Alex,' she greeted him coldly, leaving him in no

doubt as to her reaction to his presence, and to her irritation, he smiled.

'It's Ferry, isn't it?' he added, turning to her companion. 'Jason Ferry? You probably don't remember, but we met once at a charity gala. You were with Yvonne Hemmingway, and I was with her cousin, Meryl French. I'm Alex Seton. Isabel was married to my cousin.'

Jason was forced to get to his feet then to shake hands with the other man, and Isabel's nerves tightened. It wasn't like Alex to be so civil, and she couldn't help but suspect his motives.

She hardly heard what Jason said in response, but then Alex turned to her again. 'I hope you don't mind me barging in like this,' he said smoothly. 'But my uncle and I were just talking about you. We wondered if you'd—both—like to join us for a drink.'

Isabel stared up into his lean, sardonic face with unconcealed disbelief. 'You can't be serious!'

'Why not?' Alex's eyes were dark and enigmatic. 'Just because you're no longer family doesn't mean we can't be friends. I realise we've had our differences in the past, but that's over now. We—that is, Uncle Robert and I—want to mend bridges. Can't you at least meet us half-way?'

Isabel caught her breath. 'I don't believe this,' she choked. 'The Setons don't mend bridges; they destroy them!'

Alex gave a convincing impression of being taken aback at this, and to her astonishment, Jason came to his aid. 'Isabel,' he said mildly. 'I think the man is only trying to be friendly.' He resumed his seat to take her hand, giving Alex an apologetic smile. 'I'm afraid she's not feeling well right now. A few moments ago, I thought she was going to faint——'

'Will you please stop talking about me as if I wasn't here?' Isabel exclaimed angrily, snatching her hand from him. Taking a deep breath, she forced herself to look at Alex again. 'Thank you, but I have no wish to share anything with either you or your uncle! I'm not sick—only sickened, if you get my meaning.'

Alex's expression never faltered, but she thought she saw a fleeting savagery in his eyes. But then, with a rueful shrug in Jason's direction, he strolled back to his own table, leaving Isabel with the unpleasant task of explaining herself to her escort.

'Well,' he said, as soon as Alex was out of earshot. 'That wasn't very sensible, was it? And why didn't you tell me your ex-husband was one of those Setons? My God, I assumed he was some little salesman or something.'

Isabel felt inestimably weary suddenly. 'Does it matter?' she countered, wishing Jason would just forget about it. She determinedly picked up the menu. 'We were about to decide what we were going to have to eat.'

But Jason wasn't listening to her. 'Denby Textiles,' he was saying wonderingly. 'They have their own catalogue, you know. All very exclusive stuff, especially for the American market. That's one contract the Ferry agency could use.'

'No, Jason.' Isabel was quite definite now, and he pulled a wry face.

'No?'

'That's what I said.'

'Still painful, hmm?' he probed, his sharp eyes alert, and Isabel sighed.

'Just—distasteful,' she corrected him tersely. 'Now, can we talk about something else? The food, for example?'

It took an immense effort of will, but somehow she managed to swallow smoked salmon mousse and a salad. At least, she ate enough to convince Jason that whatever had disturbed her earlier no longer was a problem, and by the time they left the restaurant, she was convinced she had handled herself with aplomb.

Alex and Robert Seton had departed much earlier. She had known the minute that inimical gaze was withdrawn, and from then on it had been easier to sustain her self-assurance. She was sure now that Alex's presence in the restaurant had not been coincidental, and she hoped Jason would not object if she refused to eat there any more.

Thankfully, Jason had an afternoon engagement, and she did not have to find excuses to go home. His suggestion that they meet up later for dinner, to discuss a projected trip to Paris, was less easy to avoid, but she had left it until the last minute to demur, and Jason did not have time to try and persuade her.

'Very well. I'll see you in the studio tomorrow morning,' he conceded at last, his fair good looks marred by an angry scowl. 'And don't be late this time. Or I may just decide to terminate your contract.'

The words *Do it!* trembled on her lips, but she bit them back. It was no use letting her frustration over Alex Seton and his uncle colour her professional judgement. And that was what she was doing. Oh, Jason could be awkward, and his possessiveness where she was concerned was becoming a nuisance. But she convinced herself that she could handle him, and it would be stupid to sacrifice a well-paid occupation just to prove her independence.

She came out into Oxford Street and summoned a taxi, giving the driver her Dorset Place address before sinking back against the worn leather upholstery. It was such a relief to relax at last, and she couldn't help wondering if it was going to be worth the effort to hang on to Vinnie's shares after all. Because that was why Alex was hounding her. No matter how friendly or polite he had seemed, his real motive was plain to

see. They had intimidated her and threatened her;
Alex had even come round to the flat in an effort to
prise her legacy from her; but none of that had
worked. Her solicitors had politely, but firmly, denied
any attempt to gain possession of the shares, and now
they were trying different tactics, pretending to offer
her an olive branch.

She shook her head. Why had Vinnie done it? Why
had she pushed her gently, but firmly, back into the
middle of the ring? It wasn't as if she hadn't known
how Isabel felt about her ex-husband and his family.
In those dreadful, traumatic days, following the break-
up of her marriage, Vinnie had been her only confi-
dante, and the only person she could turn to when
she first left Nazeby. She must have known how Isabel
would feel, having to deal with Robert Seton again,
and if her intention had been to give the girl the means
to take her revenge, Isabel wished she had asked her
first before putting the onus on her.

Dorset Place ran at right angles to the road that
circled Regent's Park. Near the end of the street, the
upper windows of the converted Victorian town house,
where Isabel's apartment was situated, overlooked the
cricket ground, and the open aspect from her living-
room was one of the reasons why she had bought it.
But as well as that, it was in a reasonably quiet area,
and as she sometimes worked at odd times of the
night, she was able to sleep undisturbed during the
day. Her fellow tenants were professional people for
the most part. As Alex had taunted, they were a
conservative group, and although she knew them all
by sight, she remained an enigma to them.

It was only a little after three when she let herself
into the apartment and, kicking off her shoes, she
padded into the living-room. Then, shedding her jacket
on to the cream linen cushions of the sofa, she trod
into her bedroom, to get into something more casual.

The bedroom was the one room in the apartment in which she had allowed her imagination free rein. From the folded Chinese screen behind the bed to the adjoining cubicle with its whirlpool bath, she had spent rather more lavishly than she had intended, but the resulting blend of ancient and modern was a more than pleasing compensation. The walls were pale amber, the radiator was concealed behind a lattice-work screen, and the warm, stencilled fabric of the bed quilt was echoed in the long, draped curtains at the windows.

But today, even the beauty of her bedroom failed to lift her spirits. She was still torn by doubts about what she was doing, and troubled by the uncertain wisdom of pursuing revenge. She was not naturally a vindictive person. Until Virginia Denby had put the means into her hands, she had never thought of making Robert Seton pay for the pain and humiliation he had wreaked upon her. She didn't want to think about Chris, or Alex—and as time went by, she had begun to believe that period in her life was behind her. She had even convinced herself that she wasn't the marrying kind, and her relationship with Jason had reinforced that opinion.

Now, pulling her track suit out of the wardrobe, she stepped into the baggy yellow trousers. Then, tugging the top over her head, she rummaged for her running shoes. Her careless dressing had dislodged her hair from its knot, and she grimaced resignedly. Still, an elastic band soon secured it at her nape and, taking a deep breath, she collected her key and left the apartment.

Although it was May, it was still chilly, and though the tulips were out in the park, there were not many admirers. At this hour of the afternoon, her usual companions were children with their mothers or nannies, people walking their dogs, and a few elderly

gentlemen, out to take the air. And today was no
exception. As Isabel jogged round the lake, she saw
several faces she recognised, and her tense nerves
responded to the comfort of familiar surroundings.
She felt almost content as she trotted back across the
Broad Walk, and not until she saw the gun-metal grey
Ferrari parked outside the house in Dorset Place did
a feeling of apprehension take a hold of her.

Alex! she thought unsteadily, coming to an abrupt
halt. Or Chris? She took a ragged breath. Or maybe
just someone entirely different, she fretted. But who,
in these fairly modest apartments, was likely to own a
Ferrari? Or even know someone who did!

She sighed. Was she being absurdly melodramatic?
A car parked in Dorset Place meant nothing. Good
heavens, it could belong to anyone. Just because Alex
used to drive another expensive car was no reason to
connect the two.

Nevertheless, her pace was considerably slower as
she approached the vehicle, and only when she had
satisfied herself that it was unoccupied did a little of
the tension leave her. All the same, as she mounted
the stairs to her apartment, she couldn't help
wondering if some unwelcome visitor might not be
waiting for her outside her door.

But the landing was deserted, and she chided herself
for her own conceit. She was not that important and,
although she had been a little anxious after the way
she had snubbed Alex in the restaurant, he had more
important things to do than seek an unwilling apology.

After another reassuring look around her, Isabel
took out her key and unlocked the door. Then, letting
herself swiftly into the apartment, she carefully dropped
the latch and slid the bolt and security chain into
place. Fort Knox, she mused, a little ruefully, and
turning away from the door, she walked more confi-
dently into the living-room.

The man standing indolently in the bay of the window, staring out on to the park, turned at the sound of her approach. His shadow was the first inclination Isabel had that she was not alone, but her initial surge of panic quickly gave way to a stinging shock of resentment. 'H—how did you get in here?'

She was clutching her keys to her chest as she spoke, and Alex's lips twitched mockingly. Then, withdrawing one of his hands from the pockets of his pants, he displayed the key dangling from his fingers. 'Snap,' he said, putting it away again. 'You ought to know by now, Isabel, I can get most things I want.'

Isabel squirmed beneath his sardonic appraisal. 'I should have trusted my instincts,' she exclaimed bitterly. 'When I saw the trap downstairs, I should have known the rat would be about somewhere!'

Alex's mouth tightened a little at the deliberate insult, but he didn't respond in kind. Instead, he came round the sofa, and lowered his lean length on to the cushions. 'Thank you, I will sit down,' he declared smoothly, occupying the central position and spreading his arms out along the back on either side. 'And yes, I would like a drink, if you're having one.'

'Get out!'

Isabel could think of nothing else to say, but as she had expected, Alex didn't comply. Instead, he remained where he was, cool and relaxed, watching her frustration with bland, untroubled eyes.

Think! she told herself fiercely, when a sense of impotence threatened to overwhelm her. So long as she remained the aggressor, Alex held all the cards. He was bigger than she was; he was certainly stronger than she was; and in any verbal battle, his vocabulary would always outstrip hers. Her only chance lay in turning his anger against himself, and she wouldn't do that by stamping her feet.

'You look hot,' he said now, and she turned away

from the blatant mockery of his regard. Keep calm,
she told herself grimly. Let him think that you're
frustrated. And don't be discouraged by his attempts
to bait you.

All the same, she couldn't help being aware of him,
and not just as her tormentor either. Seated, as he
was, with the two sides of his jacket opened over a
white silk shirt and striped grey tie, she found her eyes
were drawn to the spot where one small pearl button
had parted from its fastening. The hint of brown,
muscled flesh revealed by that errant stud caused a
wave of unwelcome remembrance to sweep over her,
and she tore her eyes away before he noticed her
confusion.

'Um—is coffee all right?' she asked determinedly,
and she had the momentary satisfaction that came
from a delayed response.

'Coffee's fine,' he conceded at length, his tone just
a little less confident now, and Isabel drew a
triumphant breath as she walked into the kitchen.

Her triumph was premature. As she set the kettle
to boil, and spooned coffee into the filter, Alex came
to the kitchen door, propping his weight against the
jamb, and watching her unblinkingly. With one hand
in his pocket, and the other toying absently with his
tie, he was a disturbing presence, and it took the
utmost self-control not to spill grounds all over the
marbled working-surface.

'Why did my grandmother leave those shares to
you?' he asked unexpectedly, and Isabel felt the hot
colour running up underneath her skin. 'She must
have known how Uncle Robert would react. She was
an intelligent woman. If she wanted to leave you
something, why not money?'

Isabel refused to let his words upset her. It was a
reasonable question, after all. If she took it at face
value, she might yet retain some dignity. Why had

Vinnie left her the shares? She really wished she knew.

'I don't know,' she said now, setting out two earthenware cups and saucers. 'Do you take cream and sugar? I can't remember.'

'Can't you?' Alex straightened. 'Sugar, but no cream,' he advised her distantly. 'And you must know more than you're admitting. Was it your idea to grab a piece of Denby's?'

'My idea?' Isabel's voice rose, but she caught herself just in time. 'Of course it wasn't my idea,' she denied less vehemently, putting the sugar and cream jug on a small silver tray. 'I—would you like a biscuit? I believe there are some in the tin.'

Alex's response was to suck in his breath and turn away and, congratulating herself on her success, Isabel turned to attend to the boiling kettle. Even the fact that her hands were trembling now, and she had to dodge several scalding splashes of water, couldn't prevent her feeling of victory. If only she could keep this up, she need never fear the Setons again.

When she carried the tray into the living-room, Alex had resumed his position on the sofa. It meant that if she sat beside him, she would be uncomfortably close to his lean body, and in consequence she was forced to take the easy chair opposite. It meant that she was obliged to look at him instead of away from him, but there wasn't any alternative.

The glass-topped table between the chairs provided a suitable place to set the tray, and for the first few minutes she could direct her attention to pouring the coffee. But when that was done, and Alex's cup pushed towards him—to avoid unnecessary contact—she couldn't go on evading his gaze.

'You—er—you know Jason?' she remarked, with what she hoped was casual interest, and Alex inclined his head.

'Slightly,' he conceded tersely.

Isabel's tongue touched her upper lip. 'He's a good photographer.'

'I'm sure.'

'I've worked for him for the past eighteen months.'

'Really.'

'Yes.' Isabel relaxed a little. This was going to be easier than she had thought. If she could only sustain this rather one-sided conversation until Alex had drunk his coffee, there would be no further reason for him to stay. 'We did a shoot in Scotland a couple of weeks ago. Oh—but, of course, you know that. It—er—it was fun. The weather wasn't very good, of course, but we spent the weekend in this old castle——'

'Why, Isabel?'

Alex's weary interruption momentarily silenced her, but then, licking her lips, she said innocently, 'Why what?'

'Why this charade?' he demanded, ignoring the coffee. Moving to the edge of the couch, he spread his legs, his hands linked loosely between. 'Who are you trying to hurt? Robert? Chris?' He paused. *'Me?'*

Isabel caught her breath. 'You flatter yourself!'

'Do I?' He regarded her narrowly. 'What is it they say about a woman scorned?'

'A woman scorned?' Isabel knew another surge of fury at his arrogance. The adrenalin was rushing through her blood, and she badly wanted to give in to its insistence and order him out of the apartment. But, somehow, she managed to quell her upheaval, and although she couldn't sit still under such an onslaught, she got to her feet with admirable control. 'A woman scorned,' she said again. 'Oh, Alex! How you deceive yourself!'

Alex rose then, his dark face grim with menace. 'You like playing with fire, don't you, Isabel?' he grated. 'Well, have a care. You may still get burned!'

'I'm shaking in my shoes.' In honesty, she was, but

he would never know it. 'You can't frighten me any more, Alex.'

A spasm of some emotion she couldn't identify crossed his face at her words, and then, sighing deeply, he said, 'I'm not trying to frighten you. I came here this afternoon—as I came to your table at lunchtime—to try and salvage something from the mess Vinnie has left.'

'Really?' Isabel couldn't prevent a thread of bitterness from entering her voice at his facile explanation. 'And I suppose breaking into my apartment was all part and parcel of making up!'

'I didn't break in,' said Alex between his teeth.

'I didn't give you a key.'

'No, and I knew you wouldn't have let me in if I'd come to your door uninvited.'

'Which should tell you something about the way I feel about the Setons,' said Isabel contemptuously.

Alex pushed long fingers through the silky dark hair that lay smoothly against his head. 'I don't want to fight with you, Isabel.'

'Then go away.'

'Is that what you want?'

'Is it what I want?' Isabel uttered a scornful laugh. 'How can you doubt it?'

'You won't even consider being reasonable?'

'How reasonable was your uncle?' she spat angrily. 'How reasonable was Chris?'

'So it is a vendetta,' said Alex flatly. 'Of course. I knew it all along.'

'You know nothing!'

Isabel trembled and, unable to bear his eyes upon her any longer, she turned away, walking stiffly towards the windows, and staring out at the park, which had seemed so friendly just a few minutes before. Oh God, she thought painfully, pushing one hand underneath her hair and massaging the taut muscles at the back

of her neck. Here she was, fighting with him again.
She had determined not to let him get the better of
her but, as usual, she had lost control of the argument.
He would never believe her now, if she insisted it was
not a personal matter. So far as he was concerned,
she was still fretting because Chris had divorced her.

'So I'll tell my uncle there's no chance of his
regaining the shares, shall I?' Alex enquired now, and
Isabel tensed. Then, when she made no immediate
effort to reply, he spoke again, this time from right
behind her, and she realised he had crossed the room
without her being aware of it.

'You're a fool, you know,' he said harshly, but for
once there was no trace of censure in his voice. 'The
shares can't mean anything to you, and Robert would
pay dearly to have them back again. With what he
would give you, you could live in luxury for the rest
of your life!'

Steeling herself, Isabel turned. 'Is that what you'd
do?'

They were only a few inches apart now, and
although it wasn't easy to be as close as this to him,
she sensed it was equally as unwelcome to him.

'I—yes. I guess so,' he said, and she could see the
pulse hammering away at the taut curve of his jaw.
He swallowed. 'You could at least give it serious
consideration. You could even start your own agency,
instead of working for that creep, Ferry.'

Isabel put her hands down to support herself against
the wooden sill. 'You said you hardly knew him,' she
reminded him obliquely, and Alex took an impatient
breath.

'My association with Jason Ferry is not in question
here,' he retorted tersely. 'Look, can't we just forget
the past and concentrate on the present? You may be
making a living, but you're not exactly affluent, are

you? I mean—this apartment is very nice, I'm sure, but you could do better.'

Isabel resented this statement, but right now, she was prepared to overlook it. She sensed that once again the tables had turned and, for all his brusqueness, Alex was just as aware of her as she was of him.

'Do you still live in the same apartment, Alex?' she enquired softly, conscious that her nipples had hardened during their exchange, and were now perfectly outlined against the brushed cotton of her track suit. He had noticed them, too, she was almost sure of it, though he took care to keep his gaze levelled on her face.

'Where I live is nothing to do with you,' he responded curtly, and her lips parted at this further evidence of his frustration. 'Isabel, I'm not trying to trick you. I just want you to think what you'll be giving up, and for what? The opportunity to thwart my uncle's plans for the company? He's made a pretty good job of Denby's without your help. It was on the verge of collapse when he took over. Without him, my grandmother wouldn't have had any shares to leave you. Or do you want to be responsible for the company's decline, is that it? If so, have you thought of all the innocent people who'll lose their jobs if you succeed?'

Isabel shifted a little uneasily now. 'You know, you really should use your law degree, Alex,' she said, forcing a mocking tone. 'You'd be such an asset in the courtroom. You can argue so convincingly.'

Alex held her eyes with his. 'Have I convinced you?'

Isabel swayed. 'About what?' she asked provokingly.

'About the shares,' replied Alex grimly. 'You knew what I meant. Well? What's your answer?'

Isabel lifted her shoulders. 'I'm—thinking about it,' she said, and as if noticing a speck of dust on his collar, she stretched out her hand and brushed the fine cloth.

'What the hell do you think you're doing?' he snarled, grasping her wrist and forcing her hand away from him, and her eyes widened in pained reproof.

'You're hurting me!'

'I could,' he said savagely. 'Don't tempt me!'

'Do I?' she probed artlessly, rubbing her bruised wrist, and Alex swore.

'Do you what?'

'Tempt you?' she responded, enjoying his aggravation, and without answering her, Alex turned away.

'I suggest you inform my uncle of your decision,' he declared grimly, walking towards the door, and without giving herself time to consider the advisability of what she was about to do, Isabel went after him.

Brushing past him, she reached the door before he did, and pressing her shoulders back against the panels, she faced him, as if she had some hope of delaying him by brute force.

'What's the matter, Alex?' she taunted. 'Daren't you wait for my answer yourself?'

'Don't be stupid, Isabel.' Alex halted some distance from her. 'Get out of my way!'

'Make me,' she urged, and it was only later that she realised how reckless her invitation had been.

But at the time, the uncontrollable desire to humiliate him as he had humiliated her in the past was too strong to resist. Instead of moving out of his way, she moved towards him, and he was compelled to restrain her.

'Isabel!' He said her name on a note of desperation, and taking advantage of his momentary weakness, she evaded his grasp, and reaching up, let her tongue touch the taut skin covering his jaw.

He stiffened then, his hands seeking a hold on her upper arms and propelling her away from him. And

Isabel let him, content with the progress she had made so far in proving he was not as indifferent to her as he had pretended. She had heard his quickened breathing, and the scent of heated flesh that filled her nostrils was not just her own. That musky fragrance she could smell came from Alex's skin, and she inhaled it deeply, savouring her success.

However, if she had not been congratulating herself so prematurely, she might have noticed the moment when Alex's reactions changed. As it was, the dangerous gleam that entered his eyes went unobserved, and she was still considering what her next move should be when the hands which had been forcing her away from him suddenly changed their tactics. One moment she was fighting his urge to be rid of her, and the next she was fighting an entirely different battle.

'So that's what you want,' he said harshly, jerking her towards him again. 'Well why should I object?' And before she could summon a protest, he had captured her mouth with his.

But only for a moment. Arching her back, she was able to break that offensive contact, but in so doing, she had to step backwards again. Which was not the most sensible thing to do, she realised at once, when she came up against the unyielding panels of the door. Now she had no way of avoiding him, and as she flailed wildly at his chest, he ground his mouth against hers again with evident satisfaction.

She clenched her teeth and struggled to force her knee between his legs, but he gave her no opportunity to thwart him. Instead, the weight of his body pinned her to the door, freeing his hands to encircle her throat with ever-increasing menace.

She tried to bite him, but she couldn't, and the sudden relaxing of her jaw enabled his tongue to slide between her lips. His stance shifted as the moist warmth of his invasion penetrated deep into the hot cavern of her mouth. His choking grip on her throat eased, and the hands which had previously abused her flesh now took on a sensuous appeal. It was as if he had sensed her own weakening resistance, and his hungry mouth took sustenance from her involuntary response.

With her breathing constricted by his continued assault, all Isabel could feel and taste and smell was Alex. No matter how she fought the insidious flame he was kindling inside her, his forced proximity was making her overwhelmingly aware of how easy it would be to submit. She wanted to fight him; she wanted to escape the very real threat he posed to her independence. But the truth was, the longer he held her, the less strength she had to resist him, and his physical superiority rendered all her efforts useless.

She felt his hands move away from her throat, over the quivering width of her shoulders, and down to grip her forearms just above her elbows. But this time, he didn't push her away. Instead, he brought her closer, arching her body against his and drawing her arms around his waist. And all the time, his mouth continued to devour hers, inciting her participation. No matter how she tried to sustain her resentment against him, he was gradually succeeding, forcing her to meet his need and coaxing her tongue into his mouth.

The heat of his skin through the thin silk of his shirt burned her flesh, fusing them together, and his mouth left her lips to seek the delicate contours of her cheeks. His hands brushed her breasts, taut beneath the cotton, his palms rubbing briefly over the nipples, before moving down to her waist. Her body sagged against the door behind her as one hard thigh was thrust between hers. The powerful muscles probed her womanly softness, and then his hands slid behind her back to cup the rounded curves of her bottom. She was brought even closer, the throbbing maleness between his legs pressing hard against her stomach.

'Oh, God,' he muttered, squeezing her urgently against him. 'I'd forgotten how good you were!'

It was the tormented self-derision in his voice that got to her. It wasn't so much what he said, although that was damning enough. It was the harsh reminder in his tones that he had not instigated this that brought her to her senses. Instead of controlling the situation, she was being controlled and, taking advantage of his sexually-induced weakness, she tore herself out of his arms.

'Get out!'

She practically screamed the words at him, but although Alex was still at the mercy of his senses, he was not incoherent. 'It's a bit late for that, isn't it?' he enquired, fixing her with a lazily mocking gaze. He was making no attempt to hide his arousal from her, and when he ran his fingers down the length of his zip, she actually shuddered.

'I said—get out!' she repeated grimly, uncaring of what interpretation he might put upon it. He was still dangerously attractive to her, and it was taking all her strength to maintain her composure.

'Very well.' Alex took a deep breath and straightened his spine. Then, mocking her attempts to belittle him, he added, 'Did you come to a decision about the shares?'

'You—you bastard!'

'Is that a yes or a no?'

Isabel quivered. 'God—how I hate you, Alex!'

'Well, I guess that's a no,' he remarked, walking indolently towards the door. 'I'll pass your message on.'

She struggled to find a suitable rejoinder while he released the security locks she had set earlier, but it was useless. There was nothing she could say which would give her any satisfaction whatsoever, and when the door banged behind him, she was left with the unpleasant awareness that once again he had made a fool of her.

CHAPTER FIVE

ISABEL stepped into a slim-fitting navy skirt, and searched for the zip. It didn't help when she caught the hem of her cream silk shirt in the fastener, and she was swearing softly to herself when Lauren Bishop entered the dressing-room.

'Temper, temper,' she reproved lightly, kicking off the high heels she was wearing and bending to massage her aching feet. 'You've told him now, and he's accepted it. Think positively, Isabel. Helen, for one, is delighted to be going to Madrid in your place. Jason will get over it. You know he always does.'

Isabel sighed. 'But I told him last week that there was a board meeting on Thursday. He can't have forgotten. Jason doesn't forget things like that.'

'Perhaps he hoped you'd give it a miss,' said Lauren carelessly, leaning towards the mirror to examine her complexion. 'Do you think this foundation really suits me? Maxine says it does, but I'm not so sure.'

'Maxine says what Jason wants her to say,' said Isabel tensely, in no mood to spare the other girl's feelings. 'And how can I give the meeting a miss? I have to be there to know what's going on.'

Lauren sighed, and turned to rest her hips against the vanity unit. She was a tall girl, too, and although she was much darker than Isabel, they could wear the same colours quite successfully. They were not close friends; Isabel's attitude did not encourage close friendships. But they were compatible, and whenever they travelled abroad, they generally shared a room.

Now, Lauren shook her head. 'Why is it so important to you to actually attend?' she asked. 'I mean, you can always get a report of the meeting, can't you? Don't they take minutes or something?

Isabel sighed. 'Yes, they take minutes.'

'There you are then.'

'But I want to be there. It's—important to me to be there. It's what Lady Denby would have wanted.'

'Lady Denby,' echoed Lauren, nodding. 'She's the old lady who left you the shares, isn't she?'

'That's right.' Isabel bit her lip, and then added reluctantly, 'She was my ex-husband's grandmother.'

'Ah.' Lauren made a gesture of understanding. 'How unique!'

'Unique?'

'Yes.' Lauren regarded her wryly. 'Most in-laws do not leave their granddaughters-in-law legacies. Much less ones who are divorced from their grandsons.'

'Oh!' Isabel felt herself colouring. 'No—well, Vinnie and I were friends, you see.'

'Vinnie?'

'Lady Denby.'

'I see.' Lauren moved her shoulders as if she didn't really. 'So, you'll see your ex-husband on Thursday then.'

Isabel hesitated. 'I expect so,' she said at last. That was one eventuality she was not looking forward to.

'Is that why Jason is so peeved about it?' queried Lauren shrewdly, and at Isabel's startled look, she added, 'We all know how he feels about you, Isabel. He's not exactly made a secret of it.'

'Oh.' Isabel shook her head. 'I don't know. I hope not. I like Jason but——'

'—but he's not your ex-husband, hmm?'

'No!' Isabel was vehement. 'No, it's nothing like that. There's no question of Chris and I—that is, well—it was a mistake. Our marriage, I mean. It should never have happened. I—I was young—and flattered, and——' she bent her head to locate her shoes, '—it seemed a good idea at the time.'

Lauren frowned. 'How long were you married?'

'Two years.'

Isabel was offhand now, but Lauren was intrigued. 'So what happened? Was there someone else?'

Isabel straightened. It was to avoid questions like these that she had kept herself aloof. 'Someone else?' she asked, in her most distant voice, and Lauren sighed.

'There was a divorce,' she reminded her ruefully. 'OK,' she could see Isabel didn't want to talk about it, 'forget I asked. For a moment there, I forgot who I was talking to.' She turned away. 'I guess I'd better get changed.'

Isabel picked up her shoulder-bag and then regarded the other girl's back with some misgivings. The temptation to confide in Lauren was appealing, but the habit of keeping her own counsel was hard to break. In any case, much as she liked Lauren, the other girl was not known for her discretion, and Isabel had no desire for her private affairs to become common knowledge throughout the agency. So, with a casual 'Have a good trip!' she left the studio, deliberately using the back entrance to avoid another confrontation with Jason.

She was free now—for a week anyway, she reflected gratefully. On Wednesday, Jason, Lauren, Helen Rogers and two of the other girls were flying to Madrid on the photographic assignment Isabel had had to refuse. They would be away for five days at least, and it was an important break for Helen, the youngest member of the party. It was Isabel's turning down of this opportunity which had been the cause of her quarrel with Jason that afternoon. But Isabel had refused to be intimidated by his threats. If she lost her prime rating with the agency, then so be it. She was

determined to attend the meeting of the board of
Denby Industries, and she had warned Jason of that
fact ten days ago.

Even so, she didn't like quarrelling with him. Two
years after the divorce, she had been grateful for his
faith in her ability. A period of withdrawal, followed
by eighteen months of working at dead-end jobs, had
almost convinced her she would never be lucky enough
to work as a model again, but an interview with Jason
had set her fears at rest. He had seen the potential,
which had barely flourished at the time of her marriage,
and with his skill and guidance, she had overtaken
her youthful promise. That was why it was so hard to
disappoint him. That was why she hoped their relationship was not going to become a problem.

Thinking now about Thursday's board meeting,
Isabel realised she had less than two days to read all
the literature she could find about both Denby Industries and Mattley Pharmaceuticals. So far, her
knowledge of both was sadly limited, but she intended
to remedy that without delay. She had to admit, her
decision to thwart Robert Seton's proposal to take
over the smaller company had been made without
much thought, and only recently had she realised she
might have to face questions about her opposition. In
all honesty, all she had really intended was to show
Robert Seton that she was determined to make life
difficult for *him*. Until Alex brought the subject up,
she hadn't even considered what might happen to the
employees. All the same, she couldn't believe that
blocking the take-over would make any critical differ-
ence to Mattley Pharmaceuticals. From what she'd
read in the Press, large conglomerates often put in
bids for small companies, much against those companies' wishes. Perhaps she was doing the board of
Mattley Pharmaceuticals a favour. Considering the
alternatives, she certainly hoped so.

Nevertheless, thinking about Alex certainly rekindled her faith in what she was doing. Since he had walked out of her apartment, she had suffered agonies of self-reproach, berating herself time and again for allowing what had happened to happen. She had been so sure she could handle him, so sure she could keep herself aloof from the insidious pleasure of his lovemaking. Maybe if she hadn't made him so angry he would not have attacked her so savagely. If she had only contented herself with the success she had had, instead of taunting him so recklessly, until he had completely lost his head.

And he *had* lost his head, she reflected smugly, with some satisfaction, as she drove her second-hand Mini from the studio in Greek Street to her apartment in Dorset Place. Even he could not deny that. And not for the first time, she remembered, as the unwilling memories refused to be dismissed. If it hadn't been for Alex, she probably would never have married Chris. But pride was an uneasy bedfellow, and she had had her share, the same as anybody else.

And she had been flattered when Chris Seton showed such interest in her. They had met at a media party. She had been there representing the agency for which she had then worked, while Chris had come along with a model from a rival agency. It had been quite exciting to find herself the object of his attentions, particularly when one of the Press photographers advised her who he was. Even in those days, the heir to Denby Industries was considered one of the most eligible bachelors around, and Isabel was too young to be anything but impressed.

Even so, Chris had proved to be an entertaining companion, and, in spite of warnings from friends, she had begun accepting his invitations. She hadn't been afraid of falling in love with him. Her years in the children's home had taught her not to give her affections too freely, and although she had liked Chris, she hadn't meant to take him seriously. But that was before she met his father—and his cousin, Alex—and from that moment on, she had been running for her life . . .

The library did not yield much information about Mattley Pharmaceuticals. There was plenty of literature about Denby Industries, and its parent company, Denby Textiles, but the smaller concern warranted only a brief résumé in business directories, with no details at all about the number of employees or their plans for development. The directors' names were given, and she did contemplate contacting one of them and asking their opinion. But she could hardly ask a complete stranger to give her details of his company's policy, particularly as the merger might well be to his advantage.

What she was grateful for was the fact that the board meeting would take place in Denby Industries' London office. The company's headquarters were just off the Strand in a tall, skyscraper building with its name carved above the smoked-glass doors. Robert Seton, she knew, had his suite of offices on the penthouse floor, and the boardroom opened from them, with deliberate precision.

By Thursday morning, Isabel was half wishing she had decided to sell the shares. She could have saved herself so much soul-searching, she thought impatiently, pouring herself a glass of orange juice in lieu of breakfast. What was she going to gain by putting herself through this ordeal? Perhaps Vinnie had expected her to sell the shares. Maybe it had been her way of ensuring she was given some compensation at last.

But, somehow, Isabel knew the old lady had expected more than that. If she had wanted her to inherit a substantial sum of money, she would have arranged her will that way. No, for some reason best known to herself, Vinnie had wanted her to maintain her connection with the company. And if there was an ulterior motive, no doubt it would expose itself in time.

Isabel dressed with especial care for the meeting. She did have a momentary aberration, when she considered wearing something so outrageously provocative that the other board members would be too shocked to concentrate on what they were doing, but the inclination passed. Behaving outrageously would simply prove to Robert Seton that she was incapable of making a rational judgement, and give him the ideal opportunity to belittle her to the board. To succeed in the task she had set herself, she must first convince her peers of her sincerity. And to do that, she must not give her adversary any reason to undermine her efforts.

With this in mind, she chose a slim-fitting skirt suit in fine, beige-flecked wool, with only a rather modest slit at the back. She teamed it with an amber-coloured silk shirt and a matching tie. The severe cut of the suit was exactly what she was aiming for, and if it served to accentuate her femininity, so much the better. High-heeled bronze pumps completed the outfit, and with her hair strictly confined in a tapering knot, she was pleased with the image she had created. All the same, her hand shook a little as she followed the downward sweep of her cheekbones with a beige blusher. She still had to face Chris and his father and, for all her brave pronouncements, she was definitely apprehensive.

She took a taxi to the meeting, deciding she could not face the harassment of driving in the city this morning. A uniformed doorman opened the swing-door at her approach, and then she was inside the Denby Building, facing a bank of steel-clad lifts, like a prisoner about to serve a sentence. Stop panicking, she told herself fiercely, stepping into the first lift that opened. What have you got to lose? None of them can hurt you now.

The lift remained empty until the tenth floor when two young secretaries joined her. But they paid her scant attention, evidently absorbed with some gossip of their own making, and not until Alex's name was mentioned did Isabel feel a sense of unease.

'Well, I've heard he divorced her because she was having an affair with his cousin,' one of the girls was saying as they entered the cubicle. Then, observing Isabel's presence, she lowered her voice accordingly. 'You know who I mean, Tracy. You've seen him. Alex Seton!'

'Really!' The other girl's eyes widened, as Isabel absorbed what they were saying with hastily concealed disbelief. 'Do you think it's true?'

'I don't know.' Her companion grimaced expressively. 'But I wouldn't mind having an affair with him myself. It's a pity he's not Mr Seton's son. Imagine looking like that, and owning all this!'

'Well . . . Mr Chris isn't so bad,' murmured Tracy, hugging the pile of files she was clutching to her. 'And he does say hello, if you meet him in the building. He's not stand-offish or anything. He's really rather sweet.'

'But he's no Mel Gibson, is he?' exclaimed the first girl drily, and then, realising she had allowed her voice to rise again, she added, barely audibly, 'Besides, I've heard——'

But what she had heard, Isabel was doomed not to hear. The lift doors had opened at the fifteenth floor, and the two girls stepped out. Which was just as well, she thought tensely, catching sight of her own slightly flushed features in the mirrored panel opposite. She had had little difficulty in identifying herself as the guilty divorcee they were discussing, and while it was easy to dismiss their words as gossip, it was disturbing to realise that she was once again the target for careless talk.

The lift reached the eighteenth floor only seconds later, and Isabel wished she had had the sense to stop it at the floor below. She could have done with a few more minutes to compose herself. As it was, someone was waiting to get in, and she was obliged to step out into the reception area bordering Robert Seton's penthouse suite of offices.

Any possible excuse she might have made to give herself time to recover had to be rejected when she was recognised. The plump little receptionist who vetted all visitors to Mr Seton's office identified Isabel at once, and coming round her desk, she gave her a friendly smile.

'Mrs Seton!' she exclaimed, ignoring the fact that Isabel and her ex-husband had been divorced for almost two years. 'It's lovely to see you again. How are you? You're looking well.'

Isabel took a deep breath and went to meet her. 'It's *Miss* Ashley,' she corrected her lightly, not wanting to be reminded of her reasons for being here. 'And it's good to see you, too, Susan. Still working hard, I see.'

'As ever,' agreed Susan Lightfoot, giving a rueful shrug. 'We can't all lead exciting lives like you, Mrs—*Miss* Ashley. I see your picture in newspapers and magazines all the time. It must be lovely to be famous. But, I'm afraid, that's not for me.'

Isabel smiled, aware that Mrs Lightfoot was not as ingenuous as she appeared. She had been with Robert Seton too long to harbour any love for his ex-daughter-in-law, and although her comments seemed innocuous enough, there was an underlying note of disapproval running through them.

'Can I get you some coffee?' the woman asked now, inviting Isabel to take a seat while she informed her employer of her arrival, but Isabel demurred.

'Wouldn't it be easier if I went straight through to the boardroom?' she suggested, her fingers unconsciously tightening about her handbag. 'I am expected.'

'Oh, yes, I know.' Susan Lightfoot was not dismayed. 'But the other members of the board haven't arrived yet, and Mr Seton is busy just now.'

Isabel expelled her breath evenly. 'I think I'd prefer to wait in the boardroom,' she insisted, refusing to be kept waiting here like some interviewee. She wondered what Lady Denby would have done in such a circumstance, and then sighed. Vinnie had not been the kind of person you kept waiting. No doubt if she was here, her son-in-law would have rushed to meet her.

Susan looked taken aback but, short of interrupting her employer while he was dictating, there was little she could do. Besides, Isabel could see her arguing with herself, what possible harm could there be in allowing the newest member of the board to familiarise herself with her surroundings? It wasn't as if there were any confidential papers lying around.

'Very well,' she said at last, and indicating that Isabel should follow her, she led the way along the thickly carpeted corridor. Isabel knew the way for herself, but she allowed Mrs Lightfoot this particular indulgence, stiffening automatically when they passed the door to Robert Seton's office. His voice, as he dictated to his secretary, penetrated even those solid walls, and she mentally steeled herself for the confrontation to come.

The boardroom was large, but not excessively so. The long rectangular table was set about with fourteen ladder-backed chairs, and at each place there was a spotless white blotter, with a jotting pad and a ball-point pen for making notes.

'I'll let Mr Seton know you're here,' Susan declared as she departed, her voice decidedly frosty now. How not to make friends and influence people, thought Isabel wryly, as the door closed behind her. But if she let someone like Susan intimidate her, what chance would she have with Robert Seton himself?

Putting down her handbag on the table, Isabel controlled the stirrings of panic that gripped her by strolling the length of the room. It was quite a pleasant room, and with a watery sun streaming through the windows, it was not too formidable. The walls were mostly bare, though there was a portrait of Robert Seton at one end of the room. Isabel guessed it was situated above the chairman's position, so that even if he wasn't present at a meeting, his presence could still be felt.

Apart from the portrait, which Isabel considered to be a rather flattering likeness, there was a cabinet displaying the various awards for industry Denby's had accumulated over the past thirty years. Since Robert Seton became chairman of Denby Industries, thought Isabel contemptuously. There was no evidence here that the company had existed at all before the 1950s, and without that earlier nucleus, there would have been no company for the Setons to manage.

To one side of the room, a polished cabinet supported a coffee-maker and a dozen or more porcelain cups and saucers. Cream and sugar resided in matching porcelain containers, and a huge jug of Cona coffee simmered on its stand. Evidently, this was for the use of the board members, Isabel decided and suddenly feeling the need for sustenance, she poured herself a cup.

She was sipping the hot black liquid when the door behind her opened again, and turning with the cup in her hand, she saw her ex-husband standing in the aperture. She didn't know who was the most surprised, herself or Chris. But evidently Mrs Lightfoot had not been around to warn him that their unwelcome visitor had arrived.

And yet, surprisingly enough, Isabel was not as disconcerted by his appearance as she had expected. Somehow, he had never seemed as much to blame as his father and Alex, and although she had once despised him, she could not say she hated him.

'Didn't Susan tell you I was here?' she asked now, as he hovered in the doorway, clearly undecided on his course of action, and Chris shook his head.

'She wasn't at her desk,' he said, making a decision and advancing into the room. 'I—er—see you're having coffee. I could do with some of that myself.'

'White? With two spoons of sugar?' suggested Isabel, picking up the coffee-pot as he closed the door behind him, and Chris nodded.

'You remembered!' he exclaimed, and then his fair skin suffused with colour. 'I mean—well, it's good to see you again, Isabel. I've often wondered how you were doing, but I guessed from what Vinnie told us that you wouldn't welcome my asking.'

Isabel shrugged. It was difficult to sustain any animosity towards him. 'It's all water under the bridge, Chris,' she said, adding sugar to his cup. 'We each have our own lives to lead. Isn't that what Vinnie would have said?'

Chris took the cup she offered him with a rueful laugh. 'Well, anyway,' he added, 'you look jolly fantastic! The pictures I've seen of you don't do you justice. If you don't mind me saying so, of course.'

Isabel's expression was ironic. 'Why should I mind?' She smiled. 'You've gained a little weight yourself.'

'Haven't I just!' Chris grimaced. 'You don't have to tell me. It's the bane of my life!'

'Not so much a cherub; more a satyr!' remarked

Isabel lightly, reminding him of a joke they had once shared, and Chris groaned.

'I guess what I need is a good woman to keep me on the straight and narrow,' he joked, without thinking, but Isabel's smile disappeared.

'Do you?' she countered, meeting his eyes directly, and then, seeing the uncertainty there, she quickly looked away.

'I say—let's not get into all that,' Chris protested following her over to the windows, and standing beside her as she looked down on the panorama of the city far below. 'Dammit, Isabel, you know I'm not my own master. Never have been. God——' he swore '—I wish I were more like Alex! At least he knows what he wants out of life!'

'Don't say that.' Isabel looked up at him unwillingly, and then shook her head. 'Don't *ever* compare yourself unfavourably to Alex! At least you can't be blamed for what you are. Alex is completely without conscience!'

'But I thought you admired Alex.'

'I know what you thought, and I let you go on thinking it.' Isabel sighed. 'But I wanted out of this family, Chris. I had to get out or lose whatever self-respect I had left.'

'Bravo!'

The mocking salute and the smattering of applause that went with it brought Isabel round with a start. She had been so wrapped up in what she was saying, she had half forgotten where she was. And, in those few moments, Robert Seton had come through the connecting door from his office, and was now standing watching them with narrow-eyed malevolence.

But it was not the chairman of Denby Industries who held Isabel's attention. Even as she steeled herself to face his cold antagonism, another man came into the room behind him. Tall and dark, dressed in a lightweight business suit that complemented his tanned complexion, he moved easily to stand beside his uncle, and seeing them together, Isabel thought how similar they were.

'You don't mind if Alex joins the meeting, do you, Isabel?' Robert Seton inquired, coming towards her, his hand outstretched. His initial hostility at finding his son and his son's ex-wife together had melted in the heat of his success in confusing her, and now his palm closed about her cold hand with unconcealed satisfaction.

Isabel withdrew her fingers immediately however, clasping the hand he had touched inside the other, as if his touch had burned her. He was totally unscrupulous, she thought angrily, annoyed with herself for allowing him any advantage. The only way she could hurt Robert Seton was through his company. All other avenues had been closed to her.

Alex made no attempt to greet her, other than a faint raising of his eyebrows. Instead, he went and helped himself to some coffee, surveying the other occupants of the room with mild insouciance. Like Robert Seton, he was completely in control of his actions, and Isabel wondered if he had told his uncle about their confrontation at her flat. It she had believed that by relating that particular incident to Robert Seton she could gain some advantage, she would have done so. But she was very much afraid she would only make a fool of herself, and in spite of her antipathy towards Alex, she was not prepared to take that risk.

'So—isn't this nice?' Robert remarked, giving his son an encouraging pat on the back. 'Together again after all this time. I hope Vinnie can see us. She's certainly got what she wanted.'

Isabel took a deep breath, and then, ignoring the faintly anxious look on Chris's face, she said, 'I wonder if she'd be so happy if she knew how you'd tried to thwart her wishes, Mr Seton.' And, encouraged by the calmness of her tone, she added, 'I'm so sorry I had to refuse your generous offer for the shares she left me. But I felt I owed it to Lady Denby to abide by her decision.'

Robert's face darkened. 'Don't try to fool me!' he snapped. 'We all know how you were able to twist the old lady round your finger! You care nothing for Denby Industries. You're only interested in yourself. And whatever her doctors say, no one will ever convince me Vinnie knew what she was doing when she left her shares to you. My God, she must have had a brainstorm! You're not even *family!*'

Isabel's face was burning now, and before she could find words to repudiate his accusation, Chris chimed in. 'Don't upset yourself, Father!' he exclaimed, moving closer to his parent, as if to demonstrate his support. 'Isabel isn't going to change her mind and sell you the shares if you persist in railing at her. You should try a little psychology. That's what I'd try to do.'

Isabel's lips curled. 'Is that why you've been so nice to me, Chris?' she enquired, stung by the way he had apparently changed sides. 'I should have known you had a motive. You always hedged your bets.'

'I don't think any of us is going to achieve anything by indulging in pointless argument,' inserted Alex abruptly, setting his coffee cup aside and pushing his hands into his pockets. 'Whatever our individual feelings might be, my grandmother did choose to leave the shares to Isabel, and instead of wasting time debating the point, we should be trying to convince her that the Mattley deal would be providential to all concerned.'

CHAPTER SIX

'WELL—we did it!' declared Robert Seton triumphantly, entering his office some time later, and flinging himself delightedly into his chair. 'Alex, my boy, you're a genius! I've said it before and I'll say it again, and I insist that you let me buy you dinner this evening.'

'Yes, Alex, you did awfully well,' echoed his cousin, following them into the office. 'You really had her tied up in knots. By the time it came to the vote, she hadn't a leg to stand on!'

'I merely explained what it would mean to the staff of Mattley Pharmaceuticals if the merger folded,' said Alex flatly, not enjoying his sudden notoriety, but his uncle wouldn't let it rest there.

'It was *how* you told her, Alex,' he said, reaching for a cigar and rolling it experimentally beside his ear. 'Chris is right. She was all tied up in knots. She knew if she'd opposed it then, she'd have had the share-holders to contend with.'

'Well, perhaps if you'd taken the time to explain the situation to her, you'd never have reached an impasse,' retorted Alex, flexing his shoulder muscles wearily. 'It seems to me there's been a lack of communication on both sides. When it came to the crunch, she saw reason.'

'And do you think she'd have listened to me?' demanded Robert Seton forcefully, abandoning his relaxed position and swinging himself forward in his chair. 'Dammit, man, we both—that is, the three of us,' in deference to his son, he included Chris, 'know it was your eloquence that swung it. Don't belittle your achievement, Alex. You saw what had to be done, and you did it. And, if you caused her some bad moments in the process, so much the better.'

Alex pushed his hands into the waistline pockets of his trousers. 'What is that supposed to mean, exactly?'

'Dad's only pointing out that Isabel started this fight, not us,' exclaimed Chris, defending his parent, and Alex's mouth compressed.

'As I understand it, we set the wheels in motion when we tried to buy back the shares,' he returned, with abrasive logic. 'Perhaps if we hadn't shown our hand so openly, the question of whether or not the Mattley deal should go through wouldn't have become an item.'

'You don't believe that!' Chris gave a scornful gasp. 'My God, you were as peeved as any of us when Grandmother's will was announced! And after what she tried to do to you——'

'Just stop there, will you?' said Alex quietly, the moderation of his tone in no way detracting from its menace. 'You weren't exactly showing total disinterest when your father and I interrupted you earlier. What were you saying to her then, I wonder? She seemed to think she might have had your support.'

'That's not true!' Chris was looking hot under the collar now, and he moved about the room restlessly, searching for a suitable rejoinder. 'She—Isabel, that is—she was trying to enlist my help. Of course, I explained where my obligations lay; that naturally I supported Father's stand on the shares, and so on. But that didn't stop her making up to me. In fact, if you and Dad hadn't come in as you did, who knows what might have——'

'That's a lie!'

Before he could finish what he was saying, Alex's hand shot out and grasped a rough handful of his cousin's shirt front. Chris's neatly tied cravat was pulled out of his collar, and his face suffused with colour at the sudden constriction in his breathing. Alex's grip was lethal, and in seconds Chris was gasping for air.

'For pity's sake, Alex!' Robert left his seat to circle the desk and prise the two men apart. 'Why are you so touchy about what Chris says about that woman? Dammit, she's caused nothing but trouble ever since she became involved with this family! You can't expect Chris to be tactful. Not after what she did to him!'

Alex's jaw was hard. 'I'm sorry,' he muttered, smoothing a hand through his hair and turning away. 'I guess I'm just sick of this whole damn business!'

'Aren't we all?' sniffed his cousin, his hands shaking as he struggled to put his clothes to rights. 'There's no need to take your frustration out on me! Just because you're stung that Vinnie didn't leave those shares to you!'

Alex turned then, but his uncle was between them. 'That will do!' he exclaimed angrily. 'Chris, you'll take back that remark or you'll pay your own bills in future. Alex, we're all in something of a state at the moment. Let's cool it, shall we? And I still haven't had your answer about dinner this evening.'

Alex took a deep breath. 'I'm afraid I can't make it, Uncle,' he said, forcing a note of regret into his voice. 'I've—er—I've got a client to see at eight-thirty. I'm sorry, we'll have to make it some other time.'

'Then how about coming down to Nazeby at the weekend?' suggested Robert eagerly. 'You didn't make it last weekend, so how about this week instead? I'm not expecting any visitors. There'll just be ourselves. It would give us a chance to play a round of golf.

Maybe even take the boat out, if the weather's good.'

Alex sighed. 'I don't know . . .'

'What about me?' Chris demanded peevishly. 'Am I invited, too? Or is this just a tête-à-tête?'

'Don't be such an ass!' His father rounded on him impatiently. 'Nazeby is your home, isn't it? When have you ever not been welcome there?' He breathed heavily. 'But, as I recall it, you told me you were going to Newcastle; to the races. Or have you changed your mind about that, too?'

'What do you mean—*too?*' Chris blustered. 'Am I to understand you believe Alex's version of my conversation with Isabel, not mine?'

Robert shook his head. 'I didn't say that.'

'Not likely.'

'Look, I've got to go,' said Alex abruptly, not prepared to get involved in any more argument. 'I'll ring you later about this weekend, Uncle. If I can get away, I'll let you know.'

He felt a definite sense of relief when he came out of the Denby building. The clouds which had hung around earlier that morning had all cleared away and, like his mood, the sky was considerably lighter. It was warm, too, the first really seasonable warmth of the summer, and he decided to walk to his office instead of taking a taxi, as usual.

Half-way there, however, he was beginning to regret his enthusiasm. Walking gave him far too much time to think, and the avenue his thoughts were taking was not one he preferred. He didn't want to think about the morning's meeting; he didn't want to think about his feelings, when he had seen Chris and Isabel together; but most of all, he didn't want to think about Isabel herself, and how defeated she had appeared at the end of his cross-examination. She herself had said, just recently, that his skills as a barrister were being wasted. Well, perhaps they were. But that was no reason to feel guilty because he had used his courtroom logic to make her look a fool.

He sighed, looking bleakly about him, trying to find something to divert his troubled intellect. But the young women in their summer dresses, and the older ones, pushing toddlers in their chairs, only reminded him of what might have been, and how devastated he had been when he had first met Isabel. How many years was it now since he first saw her at Nazeby? Five? Six, maybe? Long enough, certainly, for him to have forgotten that first meeting; long enough to throw off the shackles of the past and put what had happened behind him.

The fact that that first glimpse of his cousin's future wife was still as sharply etched in his mind as ever caused him no small sense of irritation. He wanted to forget it—and her—but circumstances just kept getting in the way. Of course, until Vinnie died, it had been just a rather annoying memory, which raised its head from time to time, but which mostly he could keep under control. Since the divorce, it had become progressively easier to keep such thoughts at bay, and although he had kept himself informed of Isabel's whereabouts, and what she was doing, if ever he felt himself softening he had had only to think of Chris.

Vinnie's contact with her had made this easier, although his grandmother had never discussed Isabel with him, except in the most impersonal terms. Nevertheless, he was aware of their regular meetings, and if ever he felt the urge to update his mental dossier, it had been a simple matter to ask a perfectly innocent question.

His grandmother's death had changed many things, not least Isabel's status within the family. By leaving her the shares, Vinnie had successfully involved her grandson's ex-wife in Denby—and Seton—affairs, for years to come. She had made a mockery of Alex's determination never to see Isabel again, and locked the door, once and for all, on those halcyon days when he hadn't thought about her at all.

Now, he was uncomfortably aware that he was thinking about her far too much. If he hadn't felt the need to see her again after that disturbing scene at the flat, he would never have allowed his uncle to persuade him to attend the meeting that morning. He was quite capable of refusing his uncles's requests, and he had known at the time that by giving in to Robert, he was actually giving in to himself. But he had wanted to see her again. He had had an uncontrollable urge to go there and convince himself that what had happened between them couldn't happen again. And then, Robert had opened the door into the boardroom. Alex's blood still pounded in his temples when he remembered the scene they had interrupted, Isabel and Chris, standing closely together, deep in conversation, their nearness so reminiscent of that day at Nazeby, when Alex had come upon them in the library . . .

It had been a summer day then, too, only there had been a storm earlier in the day, and the air was still damp and thundery when Alex drove down from London. He had been in a good mood, he remembered. His interview with Storey and Heathcliffe had gone well, and he'd had every expectation of being appointed to their staff. An expectation which had later proved conclusive, when Arnold Heathcliffe had called him with the news that he had got the job.

He had walked into the house, which he had always regarded as his home, looking for either his uncle or his grandmother, with whom to share the news of his appointment. But instead of finding Robert, or his grandmother, in the library, he had found Chris and his new girlfriend, the importunate young woman his uncle had spent the last six weeks complaining about.

Alex had convinced himself that it had been because of his uncle's professed dislike of the girl that he himself had felt such an immediate aversion to the scene that confronted him. Seeing her there, with his cousin, should not have affected him at all; but it had. He had known a sudden, and totally unfamiliar, surge of animosity towards both of them, and the feeling was so powerful, he had found it difficult to be polite.

Looking back, he doubted Chris had noticed anything amiss. His cousin had never been particularly perceptive, and he had been so eager to introduce Isabel to Alex, he had apparently overlooked his reluctance.

To be honest, Alex had to admit that Isabel was nothing like what he had expected. After hearing his uncle's derogatory remarks about her success as a fashion model, he had been prepared to meet either a busty blonde or a hard-faced brunette. That Isabel was neither was immediately obvious. She was tall, and slim, and the colour of her hair defied description. It was a tumbling mass of dark red curls, shorter than she wore it now, but decidedly feminine. Her skin was flawless, a combination of apricot cream and smooth alabaster. Her mouth was wide, her nose prominent, but attractive none the less; and her eyes were a hazy, smoky-grey, with long, curling lashes tipped with gold. And when she spoke, her voice was soft and musical, and just a little husky. Chris was evidently infatuated with her, and Alex couldn't exactly blame him.

His own reactions were less easy to diagnose, but, in the days and weeks that followed, when it became apparent that Chris was determined to marry the girl, he found himself taking Robert's side in any argument. For some reason, the idea of his cousin being married to Isabel disturbed him more than he cared to admit, and if he had been able to change Chris's mind, he would have done so without hesitation.

But for once, Chris was digging in his heels and refusing to listen to either his father or Alex. He was in love, or so he said, and if his father chose to cut him off without a penny, he still intended to make Isabel his wife.

Vinnie, Alex's grandmother, was less unequivocal in her views. She like Isabel. She liked her very much. But, surprisingly, she did not actively encourage the marriage, even though, when it happened, she did give them her blessing.

Eventually, Robert Seton had given in. For all his faults, he did care deeply for his only offspring, and the wedding date was set for the autumn. Alex thought his uncle had become resigned to the prospect of becoming a grandfather in the fullness of time, and only Alex was left to accept the inevitable.

Then, one morning at the beginning of October, Alex received a telephone call from Chris. Could he do him a favour? he asked. He had arranged to come up to London that afternoon and pick Isabel up from the studio, but something had come up. An old schoolfriend had arrived unexpectedly at Nazeby, and Chris didn't like to turn him away without a meal. As it was Friday, and Alex was coming down for the weekend anyway, could he collect Isabel from the studio and give her a lift to Nazeby? He'd be eternally grateful, and it would save him an embarrassing scene.

Alex had no choice but to agree. What excuse could he have given, after all? He had arranged to spend the weekend at Nazeby, primarily so that the local vicar could arrange a rehearsal of the wedding. As Alex was to be best man, he had to attend, so there was no way he could invent a prior engagement.

Isabel was waiting outside the studio when he
arrived. Evidently, she had been prepared for his
arrival, for she showed no surprise when the black
Porsche he had then been driving rolled to a halt
beside her. Without allowing him the courtesy of
getting out and assisting her into the car, she opened
the door herself and slipped into the seat beside him.
The overnight bag she was carrying was wedged
between her knees and, reaching for the seat-belt, she
gave him a polite smile.

'Thank you,' she said, straightening her shoulders
against the back of the seat. 'I hope you don't mind
this imposition.'

Alex was tempted to say that it would be all the
same if he did; but he didn't. It was a good two-hour
drive to Nazeby, and for all his antipathy towards
her, he disliked the notion of starting the journey with
a row.

Instead, he dismissed her gratitude with casual indifference, making some innocuous remark about the
state of the traffic, to set their relationship on an even
footing.

Yet, for all his apparent negligence, Alex was aware
of the young woman sitting beside him with every
fibre of his being. Although his impression of her by
the roadside and getting into his car had been necessarily brief, he knew how she looked and what she
was wearing. Surprisingly enough, she had not dressed
formally for the journey. Alex guessed the thigh-
length, collarless T-shirt dress and mauve tights, were
her usual attire to and from the studios. Even her face
was scrubbed clean of make-up so that the pearly
radiance of her skin was unblemished. Only her hair
appeared a contradiction. Someone, the hairdresser at
the studio possibly, had threaded the fiery strands into
dozens of small braids. Each braid was fastened with

tiny ceramic beads, and when she moved her head too quickly, the beads chinked together. It was not an unpleasant sound, but it was unusual, and the first couple of times it happened, Alex found his eyes drawn to its source.

'Um—Chris is entertaining an old schoolfriend, isn't he?' she queried, after Alex had negotiated the traffic in central London. Like him, she was obviously endeavouring to forget their differences, for the journey, at least, and Alex made an effort to respond in equal vein.

'So I believe,' he said, immediately aware that his tone was not as cordial as hers. 'Chris has a lot of friends from his days at Haveringham.'

'Haveringham.' Isabel picked up on his last word. 'That's a public school, isn't it? I seem to remember hearing the name, but I don't know where it is.'

'It's in Buckinghamshire,' replied Alex evenly. 'It's quite a beautiful part of England. Do you know that part of the country at all? Or is London more to your taste?'

He realised his final question was decidedly patronising, but he couldn't help it. The more he spoke to her, the stronger was the urge to try and belittle her. He didn't know why that was. He only knew that her indifference infuriated him.

'No. I don't know Buckinghamshire,' she responded honestly. 'But London hasn't always been my home. I was born in Lincolnshire, as a matter of fact. It wasn't until I started working that I actually came to London.'

Alex absorbed this news with reluctant attention. Somehow, he had assumed she had always lived in the city. His assessment of her character had been so total, it was disconcerting to realise there were facets of it he had overlooked.

'What part of Lincolnshire?' he asked now, assuring himself his interest was purely circumstantial, and Isabel gave him a sideways glance.

'I'm not sure,' she admitted ruefully. 'I was brought up in a children's home, you see. I never knew my parents. Only that my mother abandoned me, when I was a few days old.'

Alex was amazed. No wonder Chris had glossed over the fact that Isabel's parents were dead and unable to attend the wedding. If Robert Seton had known that the girl was an orphan, he might well have decided to call Chris's bluff.

'Are you shocked?' she asked now, and Alex struggled to put his thoughts in order.

'Surprised,' he conceded, after a moment. Then, compulsively, 'Didn't you ever try to find out who your parents were?'

Isabel shook her head. 'No.' she paused. 'I decided that if my mother was the kind of person to abandon her own daughter, I didn't really want to know her.'

They were travelling along the M3 now, and Alex had to concentrate on overtaking a stream of slow-moving lorries at that moment, so it was several minutes before he said, 'And your father? Didn't you ever try to trace him?'

Isabel sighed. 'He probably didn't even know of my existence,' she replied. 'Eighteen years ago, people were a lot less liberal-minded than they are today. My mother may have kept my birth a secret. Is it fair now to resurrect a mistake?'

Alex lifted his shoulders. 'You're very philosophical.'

'Just practical,' she amended quietly. And then, with a little splaying of her hands, she gave a low laugh. 'I don't know why I'm telling you all this. What is it they say when they're arresting someone? "Anything you say will be taken down, and may be used in evidence against you?" Is that what you're planning to do? Tell your Uncle? Give him yet another reason to try and prevent this marriage?'

Alex cast her a cooling glance. 'If Chris hasn't chosen to tell him, why should I?'

'Because you're your uncle's favourite.' Isabel spoke without prejudice. 'Oh, you may not be his son and heir, but you're the one he depends on, aren't you? You're the one who supports him, who shares his opinion of me.'

Alex's mouth compressed. 'Which is?'

'What?' Isabel was momentarily confused.

'My opinion of you. What is it?'

'Oh——' She bent her head now, and the tiny beads chinked against the vulnerable curve of her neck. 'You don't like me. You never have. Well—the feeling's mutual. So don't bother to deny it.'

Alex's hands clenched on the wheel. 'You know nothing about me.'

'Yes, I do.' She drew a steadying breath, and looked up at him. 'You haven't exactly hidden your feelings. You think I'm marrying Chris because he's got lots of money. You despise my profession; and you criticise how I look.'

Alex's breathing was less than steady now. 'You don't have a *profession!*' he retorted at last. 'Taking your clothes off in front of a camera is hardly meaningful employment——'

'I don't take my clothes off!' Isabel was indignant.

'You would, if the price was right,' returned Alex without sympathy, and she glared at him impotently, restrained from physical retaliation by his concentration on the traffic.

Thereafter, there was silence for a while. Isabel flung herself round in her seat, so that she was facing away from him, her knees nudging the door handle, and

Alex tried to take some interest in his driving, which usually gave him satisfaction. But, for all his determination to ignore her, his eyes were irresistably drawn to the long, slender fingers, balled into fists on her knees, and the smooth shapely curve of her thigh, exposed to some advantage by the sheer tights she was wearing. The shortness of her skirt was disturbingly provocative, although he doubted if she was aware of it. She wore her clothes with the same careless elegance with which she moved. She was naturally graceful, that much he had to grant her, and the sexuality of her movements owed more to his sensitivities than to hers.

They left the motorway after Winchester, turning on to a narrower, two-laned road, and driving deep into the Hampshire countryside. They passed through villages, sleeping in the shadows of early evening, tiny hamlets some of them, with only a church and a petrol pump to mark their passing.

Alex knew his way well. There was a busier, major road he could have taken to reach his destination, but her preferred the quieter route. Besides, at this hour on a Friday afternoon, all the major roads were crammed with commuter traffic, and inhaling someone else's exhaust fumes was not the way he liked to start his weekend.

ISabel had evidently noticed their detour, however and judging by the way she was reading the road signs they passed she was no doubt wondering where he was taking her. Knowing Chris's penchant for taking the shortest route between any two points, he doubted his cousin had brought her this way. His lips twitched. Perhaps she was afraid he might be abducting her for his uncle; or planning to murder her, and dump her body in some remote corner of the county.

'It's only about twenty miles now,' he remarked, at

last, compelled, for reasons he didn't care to admit, to reassure her, and Isabel turned her smoky eyes his way.

'Is it?'

'I don't lie,' he assured her crisply, slowing as they approached a *Give Way* sign. 'This way may be a few miles further, but at least we're not hampered by slow-moving vehicles. And,' he appended almost defens-ively, 'It's a much more scenic route.'

Isabel shrugged. 'I wasn't complaining, was I?'

Alex's blood rose. 'Is it too much to expect that you might speak civilly——'

'Civilly!' Isabel hardly let him finish the word, her eyes fixed on his face in raw contempt. 'After what you've said to me?' You arrogant—bastard! If it wasn't for the fact that Chris thinks you're wonderful, I'd never speak to you again!'

Alex's foot hit the brake almost instinctively. His anger was almost choking him, and without hesitation he swung the car on to the grassy verge at the side of the road, uncaring of the fact that the waving fronds of ragwort could be hiding a ditch or worse. He was lucky. The Porsche's tyres skidded a little bit on the grass which had been dampened earlier in the day by a thunderstorm, but apart from a few bumps, the car came safely to a halt.

Then he turned towards her, his eyes blazing furiously, saying the first thing that came into his head to prevent himself from physically attacking her. 'If you feel like that, I suggest you find your own way to Nazeby!' he snarled, gripping the wheel as he'd like to grip her neck. 'Go on! Get out! I'm sure you'll find someone more to your liking to give you a lift!'

Isabel blanched. 'You don't mean that.' She glanced about her and he saw the muscles of her throat flex as she swallowed. 'I don't even know where we are.'

'We're approximately nineteen miles from Nazeby,' said Alex harshly. 'Exactly one mile further than we were when I gave you our situation. Is the prospect daunting? It shouldn't be for someone of your doubtful—talents!'

Isabel caught her breath. 'You'd do this, wouldn't you?'

'You'd better believe it.'

She sniffed. 'And what will you tell Chris?'

Alex shrugged. 'I may not *tell* Chris anything. I might just decide to waive my role in this fiasco of a wedding, and drive straight back to London.'

'You wouldn't do that.' She stared at him.

'Wouldn't I?'

Alex returned her stare without flinching, and as if he had just pushed her too far, Isabel acquiesced. 'All right,' she said, a disturbingly flat note in her voice now. 'All right. I'll take my chance.' She shook her head. 'There are such things as buses; and trains. I don't need your help to get to Nazeby.'

Thrusting open her door, she threw her overnight bag on to the verge and started after it. She really expected him to abandon her here, Alex realised, and suddenly he knew that for all his simmering resentment, he couldn't do it. What *would* Chris say? he asked himself bitterly; but it wasn't just his cousin's reactions that were causing him to have second thoughts. He couldn't leave her here, at the mercy of every tramp and sexual pervert that might come her way. Besides, the sky was still very overcast, evening was approaching, and if a storm erupted, there were too many trees around for safety.

'Forget it!' he said abruptly, putting out his hand and grasping her shoulder, preventing her from following her bag out of the car. But now, she turned on him.

'Let go of me,' she commanded, in an icy voice, though her eyes sparked fire. 'Don't you think because you're having an attack of conscience, you can manipulate me at will. I didn't ask you to give me a lift. Chris insisted on it. And, fool that I was, I thought you might actually be prepared to make friends at last. But I was wrong. I should have realised you were too much like your uncle to have a charitable thought in your head!'

Alex's mouth hardened. 'I said, forget it,' he repeated harshly. 'Now, cut out the dramatics and pick up your bag. We still have several miles ahead of us, and I want a shower before supper.'

'I'm not stopping you,' said Isabel carelessly, but she was making no attempt to reach out and pick up her bag, and with a sigh of impatience, Alex was forced to push open his own door to walk round and get it himself.

However, as soon as he released his hold on Isabel, she was out of the car in a flash and, as he first of all lunged after her, and then, finding himself baulked by the gear console, thrust his legs out of the car and came to his feet, she snatched up her bag and scrambled through a gap in the hedge into the field beyond.

'Isabel!' he yelled, his frustration knowing no bounds as he plunged after her. 'For God's sake, what the hell do you think you're doing?'

She was a hundred yards ahead of him when he emerged from the hedge, his hair almost torn from his scalp by a wayward briar. Looking down at his jacket, he saw that it too had been raked by the prickly bushes, and the cuffs of his trousers were already damp from the wet grass. When he got his hands on her . . . he promised himself savagely. But threats were not going to bring her back, and with a violent oath he went after her.

Although she had a head start, his shoes were flat-heeled and he had a longer stride. Besides, she had accidentally stumbled into the boggy surrounds of a swollen pond, and while the herd of cows that occupied the field lifted their heads in mild curiosity, Isabel's steps were dogged with cold mud. She flailed about for several seconds, like a swimmer who has suddenly discovered he's wearing cement shoes, and then she over-balanced, sinking to her knees in a morass of dirt.

Alex reached her just as she was using her hands to lever herself to her feet again, and for all his anger with her, he couldn't prevent the errant lifting of his mouth. She looked so pathetic somehow, her knees and feel all caked with mud. And funny, too; a kind of cruel retribution.

'Don't move,' he said, as she endeavoured to lift her feet out of the squelch. 'You may lose your balance again. Here,' he took some papers, a pen and his wallet out of his jacket pocket and tossed the expensive garment down on the earth between them. 'Step on to that, and come this way. 'It's dry enough where I'm standing.'

Isabel gasped. 'But your jacket!'

'I have another,' he informed her drily. 'Just do as I say. Or do you like standing in mud? If so, I'll leave you to it.'

Isabel cast him a resigned glance. 'Oh, all right,' she said wearily, lifting one foot and depositing it, not without some reluctance, on the fine silk lining of the jacket. Then, gaining courage, she lifted the other, and seconds later she was on the comparatively dry grass beside him. 'Thank you.'

Alex shook his head. 'You look a mess.'

'I know.' She looked down at herself ruefully. 'What can I do?' Then, looking up at him. 'What am I going to tell Chris?'

'What am *I* going to tell Chris?' amended Alex drily. 'We're going to have to think of something. But first of all, I suggest we do something about your hands and legs.'

'Can we?' Isabel was doubtful, and Alex found himself grinning.

'I guess so. It may have slipped your notice, but this pond adjoins a stream. Over there. With a bit of luck, the water in the stream will be clean. Cold, perhaps, but clean.'

It was. With an absence of affectation, Isabel peeled off her tights and washed them in the stream while Alex did his best to clean her shoes. Grass and dock leaves soon had the plain purple pumps looking outwardly as good as new. The lining inside remained stained, but once they were on her feet, this discrepancy would not be visible.

With her hands and feet washed clean of the mud, Isabel rose to her feet to face her rescuer. 'I'll put these in my bag,' she said, indicating the damp tights in her hand. She shivered. 'Is it very badly stained? I tried to keep it out of the mud as best I could.'

'I've brushed it down, and I guess when it's dry it'll be as good as new,' said Alex, handing her her shoes, but hanging on to the bag. 'Right. Are we ready to go? Or are you still intent on hiking to Nazeby?'

Isabel's lips twitched. 'What do you think?'

Alex felt his senses stir. 'I think we should get back to the car before someone steals that,' he replied, his tone a little cooler than it might have been because of his unexpected arousal. 'After you. And take care where you put your feet!'

Isabel carried her shoes to the car, walking easily in her bare feet. Without heels, she seemed smaller, more vulnerable somehow, and Alex had to remind himself

of who she was as his antagonism gave way to other
emotions. Her bare legs were disturbingly beautiful,
long and slender, and far too accessible below her
short skirt. He found himself staring at the rounded
curve of her rear as she scrambled back through the
hedge, and the unmistakable tightness of his trousers
betrayed his callow reaction. It was years since any
woman had had such an effect on him, and he swung
round the car irritably to avoid her observation.

This time, he stowed her case in the boot of the car
realising, as he did so, that had he done that in the
beginning, none of this might have happened. She
could hardly have gone charging off across the fields,
leaving him in possession of her belongings. Without
her purse, her clothes, she would not have felt such
independence, and he would not be suffering now
from the discomfiting effects of his frustration.

'Where's your jacket?' she enquired, as she slipped
into the seat beside him, and Alex glanced over his
shoulder.

'In the boot, with your bag,' he replied, waiting for
her to close the door so that they could be on their
way. He was eager now to reach their destination.
Eager, too, to escape the knowledge that had eluded
him for so long.

'Will it clean?' she persisted, examining her shoes
before putting her feet into them. She gave him a
rueful smile. 'You'd better send me the bill.'

'Perhaps I will.' Alex was curt, but he couldn't help
it. For Christ's sake, he fretted, why didn't she shut
the bloody door? Every second they remained here,
his control over the situation decreased.

'I've always liked these shoes,' she said instead,
surveying them affectionately, like some remarkable
find she'd made. 'I got them in Venice at Easter. Have
you ever been to Venice? Oh, yes, I suppose you must

have. Chris says you've travelled quite a lot.'

Alex sighed. 'Aren't you cold?'

'A little bit. Why?'

'Then why don't you close the door? So we can get moving.'

Isabel looked surprised. 'Oh—sorry.' She reached for the armrest. 'I'll just put my shoes on first. Then I can see what I'm doing.'

Afterwards Alex cursed himself for his impatience. He could have waited, while she bent and slid the offending shoes on to her feet, but he didn't. Instead, as she bent to accomplish her task, he leaned across her to reach the door, and when she came up suddenly, his arm was trapped behind her.

He never knew who was the most surprised: himself, for being caught that way, or Isabel, when she found his face only inches from hers. But, in either case, the result was the same, and for a heart-shuddering moment, neither of them moved. Alex found he was breathing more quickly than his exertions had warranted and, his eyes falling from Isabel's flushed, startled face to the steady rise and fall of her lungs, discovered a similar reaction in her. As he watched, the tenor of her breathing accelerated, and the rounded breasts beneath her dress swelled against the cloth. Her nipples hardened, creating little aureoles of darkness beneath the brushed cotton, and Alex's lips parted involuntarily, tempted beyond measure to discover how they would feel beneath his mouth.

Isabel spoke first, her voice several shades higher than it normally was, dragging his eyes away from her breasts and back to her face. 'No, Alex,' she got out chokily, but he could tell from the way she said his name that she was as aroused as he was.

'Why not?' he demanded, the arm behind her drawing her inexorably nearer, his hand sliding beneath her arm to touch the warm swell of her breast.

'Because we can't,' she articulated unevenly, but Alex was scarcely listening to her. The feel of her breast beneath his hand was so incredibly good, he couldn't think of anything else, and when her soft lips opened to rebuke him, his mouth took possession of hers.

She fought him at first, trying to drag her lips away from his, and pushing at his chest with her hands. She would have used her legs, too, had the console not been in the way. But Alex was deaf and blind to her pleas, intent only on satisfying the insatiable urge he had to make her as aware of him as he was of her. And he succeeded, too. Or at least, he thought he did. When she stopped fighting him, when she stopped clenching her teeth together and allowed the hot wet thrust of his tongue to slide between, Alex felt a sense of pleasure he had never felt before. The seductive cavern of her mouth offered boundless sweetness, and when her tongue entwined with his, his senses swam.

He forgot who she was, and why he was bringing her to Nazeby. The idea that she was his cousin's fiancée, and as such, forbidden fruit to him, didn't so much shame him as inflame him. She didn't love Chris, she *couldn't* love Chris, not and kiss him as she was doing. Her hands were no longer resisting him, they were curled quite confidingly against his neck. And when he let his hand trace the shape of her breast beneath the dress, she pressed herself closer, making him catch his breath.

He wanted her. God, how he wanted her! The raw possession of his tongue was no substitute for the sensual delights of imagining her tight muscles closing about his taut manhood. He was aching for her already, and he longed to take her hand and let her feel his need.

But he was very much afraid, if he did so, his control would slip completely. Time enough for that afterwards, he thought. Right now, he had other things on his mind. Thank God, it was getting dark at last. No one would observe them when they made love.

His hand moved lower, caressing the tremulous curve of her stomach, before sliding down to the provocative hem of her skirt. Isabel's legs parted willingly when his hand slipped between them, and he stroked the inner skin of her thigh, as his fingers moved even closer to the moist, scented core of her being. She smelt delicious, all warm and soft and feminine. He had to steel himself not to rush her, and he groaned when her small teeth fastened on his ear . . .

'Isabel . . .' he rasped huskily, burying his face in the hollow of her neck, hearing her beads chink together as his mouth sought the warmth of her flesh . . .

CHAPTER SEVEN

THE SUDDEN tapping on the window at his side of the car shocked them both. To his relief, as he lifted his head, Alex saw that the glass had misted over all round, so that anyone peering through it would have only a hazy impression of the two people inside. But then a torch was switched on that penetrated the condensation, and Alex swiftly turned to press the button that operated his window.

'Is everything all right, sir?'

Before he could voice a protest, a helmeted policeman bent to peer through the open window at them, eyeing the two occupants of the car with a jaundiced eye. Alex immediately felt about fifteen again, caught making love in the back of one of his uncle's Land Rovers. He had driven a Land Rover about the estate from the age of twelve onwards, and he clearly remembered his first experience of sex with the daughter of one of his uncle's tenants. She had been older than he was, eighteen or nineteen at least, but more than willing to initiate him into the arts of sexual pleasure. He had been a willing pupil, too, he remembered, as Isabel hurriedly straightened her clothes beside him; but he was not fifteen now, and Isabel was no easy conquest . . .

'I—perfectly,' he said, realising it would be unwise to complain. They were parked in a prominent position, after all, and his car had always attracted attention. He just hoped the policeman hadn't recognised its registration. All the cars belonging to the members of the Seton family were licensed with private plates, and his own was instantly recognisable to anyone who knew him.

'Are you all right, miss?' The policeman had now turned his torch on Isabel, and she shifted nervously.

'I—of course,' she answered. 'Um—I was feeling rather sick, and—and I asked if we could stop. I'm feeling much better now, thank you.'

'Good, good.' The policeman patted the roof of the car as he straightened, evidently satisfied that they were unlikely to corrupt the neighbourhood. 'OK, sir, I won't detain you any longer. Have a good evening, and remember, don't drink and drive.'

'Thanks.'

Alex's response was necessarily brief, but at least his identity was still intact, he reflected with some relief, as he started the car. And, the policeman's intervention had brought him to his senses. God! he thought incredulously. He had actually been considering making love with Isabel in the car! He hadn't made love in a car since he was at university. He must have been temporarily deranged!

Nevertheless, he was no less aware of her now than he had been before, and that knowledge ate him up. What was wrong with him? She was Chris's fiancée, for Christ's sake! Was he out of his mind?

And what about Isabel? What was she thinking? he wondered. After all, he added, struggling to justify himself, she had been as much to blame as he was. She hadn't exactly had hysterics when he touched her. On the contrary, after that first perfunctory protest, she had encouraged him, inviting him to take liberties with her, and responding with a passion he would not have believed her capable of.

His hands tightened on the wheel. Why the hell didn't she say something? She must know how he was feeling. Or was she more experienced in these matters than he was, he asked himself bitterly. Was that why he had overcome her protests so easily? Because he wasn't the first man she had played around with since her engagement?

'Will you tell Chris?' she asked at last, and Alex's lips twisted at the implied anxiety.

'Will you?' he countered, keeping his eyes on the stretch of road ahead, illuminated by his headlights.

'Of course not,' she answered, twisting her hands together in her lap. 'I—it should never have happened.'

'No.' He conceded the point, even though his senses rejected the calm summation. 'I guess it could be pretty inconvenient for you if it came out.'

'And for you,' she countered hotly. Then, 'I didn't ask you to touch me.'

'You didn't put up much resistance,' he retorted, despising himself for his inhumanity, even though he told himself he was within his rights. 'Well, don't worry. I shan't destroy Chris's perfect image of you. I'll let you do that for yourself.'

'Thank you.'

Her response was barely audible, and once again Alex felt a pig for accusing her. But what the hell, he argued silently, she deserved everything he could fling at her. She was beautiful, but she was faithless; alluring, but immoral; desirable, and totally without conscience.

Yet, in spite of his professed contempt for her, that weekend at Nazeby was the worst weekend he had ever spent. Seeing her with Chris, watching as his cousin pawed and fondled her, tore him up, and going through the motions of the wedding service was the purest kind of torment. He didn't love her, he told himself through the long nights, when the thought of her married to Chris plagued his senses, but he did want her. He wanted her so badly, he was almost prepared to destroy his friendship with Chris for ever. He had the distinct suspicion that if he went to her room and took up where they had left off in the car,

Isabel wouldn't exactly repulse him, and this knowledge did not make sleep any easier. He knew his uncle wouldn't blame him. On the contrary, Robert would have been delighted to have an excuse to cancel the wedding. Any inkling that Isabel might not be in love with his son would have caused an immediate confrontation between them, and no amount of persuasion on her part would have saved the day.

But Alex did nothing, and he said nothing, allowing the plans for the wedding to go ahead unchecked. He kept out of the way as much as possible, and eventually the weekend passed. Chris took his fiancée back to London himself, and Alex stayed on an extra day to cool his heated blood. He knew his grandmother was concerned about him, but he couldn't tell Vinnie what was wrong. Instead, he let her draw her own conclusions, no doubt assuming that, like herself, her grandson still had reservations about the following weekend.

Alex eventually went back to London on Tuesday afternoon, and spent the next three days fighting the urge to see Isabel again. But by Friday evening, the day before she was due to be married to his cousin, he had come to the end of his tether. After imbibing rather freely at the pub across the road from his office, he took a taxi to Stanton Street, and climbed the stairs to the second-floor studio flat she shared with two other girls. He was past the stage of caring who saw him, but as luck would have it, Isabel was alone, ironing the creases out of the dress she was to wear on the following day.

She answered the door to his knock, evidently expecting someone other than the slightly inebriated male who was propped against the wall outside. 'Alex!' she exclaimed, and just for a moment he thought he saw a glimmer of relief in her smoky-grey gaze. But then she realised he had been drinking, and with an exclamation of disgust, she would have closed the door to him.

But, in spite of his intoxication, Alex still had possession of his faculties and, discerning what she was about to do the moment before she did it, he moved to put his foot in the doorway, successfully blocking her attempt to shut him out.

'Now—is that any way to greet your future cousin-in-law?' he protested, pressing the heel of his hand against the door as he spoke, and propelling it inward. 'Aren't you going to offer me a drink? In—cel—celebration, so to speak.'

His tongue faltered over the word, but he could see she understood him well enough, and his lips twisted bitterly at the knowledge that even now, in shabby jeans and a loose smock, her fiery hair in wild disorder about her shoulders, she was devastatingly attractive. The tight jeans outlined the long, lovely shape of her and, remembering the warm skin beneath the denim, Alex felt a familiar quickening of his senses.

'What do you want, Alex?' she demanded now, making no attempt to fight him over the door. She acknowledged that he was stronger than she was, and would therefore win in any physical confrontation. But her attitude towards him wasn't conciliatory; it was downright contemptuous.

'What do you think I want, Isabel?' he asked, ignoring the scornful sparkle of her eyes. He closed the door behind him and leaned back against it. 'I want you, of course. And you can't deny that you want me.'

'*I? Want you?* You have to be joking!'

The derisive tone of her voice was a set-back, but Alex refused to believe she meant it. 'Am I?' he asked, moving purposefully away from the door, trapping her between a tapestry-covered couch, which had seen better days, and the ironing-board she had been using earlier. 'I don't think so. We both know what we want, and as we appear to be alone, now would seem as good a time as any.'

Isabel summoned an incredulous laugh, but there was no humour in it. 'You're crazy!' she exclaimed. 'And drunk! Go home and take a shower. A cold one, preferably.'

'Don't—make fun of me,' advised Alex harshly, swallowing back the taste of bile which had risen sickeningly into his throat. The awareness that he had drunk more than he should have done was only adding to his frustration, and he shook his head impatiently to clear his muddled brain.

'Go home, Alex,' Isabel said again, trying to move the ironing-board without overturning the iron. 'Please! You don't know what you're doing. Isn't Chris expecting you? Aren't you and he supposed to be having an evening out together?'

If she thought mentioning Chris's name would make him think again, she was mistaken, thought Alex bitterly, his hands reaching for her shoulders. Even the idea of Chris having the right to touch her as he was touching her, fired him with jealousy, and imagining them making love, filled him with disgust.

'Take your hands off me!' she exclaimed, flinching away from his fingers as they moved caressingly over her shoulders. 'Alex, for God's sake! Are you mad?' But he wasn't even listening to her.

Her bones were so narrow and delicate, so close to the surface of her skin that he could feel every hollow between. Her skin itself was soft and supple, like the thickest cream beneath his hands; and her hair brushing his fingers was fine and vital, so full of life and electricity, that he almost expected to feel a shock when he buried his face in its glory.

Oh, God! It was good to be touching her again, so good to feel her warmth against him, and the more she twisted against him, the more aroused he got. His hands slid over her shoulders and down her back, lingering in the curve of her waist before cupping her rounded bottom, and moulding her softness to him.

He lifted his head then, eager to find her mouth with his, eager to taste the sweetness of her tongue with his own. He couldn't ever remember being so excited, not even as a youth, and his growing sense of urgency was only equalled by his desire to prolong the pleasure.

The searing heat of the weight that swung against the side of his neck was devastating. Aside from the fact that it almost knocked him unconscious, the exquisite pain of the burning metal caused him to yell in agony. He didn't remember releasing Isabel, he didn't remember knocking over the ironing-board, as he clapped a protective hand over the burn and staggered back against the door. The first coherent memory he had was of Isabel staring at him in horror, while the tears poured down her face, and then her rushing towards him, desperate to tend his injury.

But Alex was sober now, stone-cold sober, his brain washed clean of any emotion but outrage by the crippling blow of the iron. For that was what it had been. He recognised that fact now; even while his subconscious protested that it really couldn't have been Isabel's hand that lifted it.

But it *had* been her hand. There was no one else there and, as if to certify his belief, she was still holding the offending article as she rushed towards him. She realised what she was doing before she reached him, of course, throwing the erstwhile weapon aside before reaching out to him with trembling hands. She was evidently as shocked by what had happened as he; though not as afflicted, reflected Alex bitterly, gritting his teeth against the pain in his neck; not as afflicted at all.

'Alex—I'm sorry!'

Her distress was palpable, but Alex had no sympathy for her. Indeed, he was wondering how he could have been so stupid as to come here in the first place. Without her air of confidence she was quite a pathetic figure, he reflected contemptuously, and unlike some women who could cry gracefully, Isabel's tears were causing her lids to swell, and the skin around her eyes to become puffy.

'Spare me!' he muttered, wincing as he took his hand away from his neck and a sliver of skin came with it. 'You knew what you were doing, and I guess I should be grateful for it. You were .right. I was drunk, bloody drunk, as it happens, or I wouldn't be here in the first place. However——' he turned towards the door, '—you certainly brought me to my senses. Put it down to experience. When a woman comes on to me, I usually try to oblige her.'

After that, the wedding was an anticlimax. Alex remembered going through the motions, as he had done at the rehearsal, without allowing any part of his emotions to become involved. The band-aid on his neck had aroused some comment from his uncle, but a dismissive remark about the razor slipping while he was shaving had successfully balked further enquiries. It was easy enough to let Robert, and Chris, think that he had not been entirely sober when he did it. And Kerry O'Flynn, who had just joined him at his apartment in London, and who had actually attended to the burn when he got home, would never have dreamed of questioning its origins. He was too well versed in diplomacy for that.

If only that had been the end of it, thought Alex now, reaching the building that housed his office with some relief, and pushing open the swing-doors. It should have been the end of it and certainly, so far as he was concerned, her marriage to his cousin had severed any connection between them. He might have been willing to cheat on Chris, so long as he and Isabel were not actually joined in wedlock, but stealing his cousin's wife was quite a different matter.

None the less, when they came back from honeymoon, his good intentions had been stretched beyond measure. Far from looking tanned and relaxed, contented after four weeks of sunning herself in the Caribbean, Isabel appeared pale and nervous, and thinner than he remembered. She hardly ever looked him in the eye and, instead of gaining in confidence, if anything she had become tense and withdrawn.

Chris, however, seemed much the same as usual. Alex's first, treacherous suspicion, that he might be to blame for Isabel's apparent unhappiness was quickly dispelled. If anything, Chris was even more attentive to her as his wife, than he had been as her fiancé, and it was obvious that if anything was wrong with their marriage, Isabel must be to blame.

Even so, he was outraged when his uncle confided in him a few months later that Isabel had suggested to him privately that the marriage should be dissolved. Her reasons, Robert said, were that she found life at Nazeby excessively boring after living in London, and Chris couldn't please her, no matter how he tried.

'Imagine coming to me!' his uncle had exclaimed savagely, when he told Alex what had happened. 'The boy's own father! As if she could expect me to take sides against my own son!'

But later, when Alex had suggested that perhaps a separation might be the best thing for all concerned, his uncle had been adamant that that was not feasible. 'I don't want the girl going back to London, telling all her friends that Chris is to blame,' he averred strongly. 'No, that's not the way, Alex. We'll have to think of something else.'

Alex had sometimes wondered why Isabel hadn't just walked out when she had first wanted to do so. Chris and his father could hardly keep her at Nazeby by force. But, apparently, according to Robert, she was holding out for a marriage settlement, something his uncle was not prepared to give to someone who had used his son so cold-bloodedly.

'There's no question about it,' he said to Alex, during one of their interminable discussions on the subject. 'She only married Chris for what she hoped to get out if it. I wouldn't care, but the boy's still as besotted as ever. He's begged me not to do anything to hurt her, and God help me, I don't know what to do!'

And then, providentially, the situation had resolved itself without his uncle having to do anything about it. Remembering this now, Alex could feel again the savagery he had felt when Robert had informed him of Isabel's actions. He hadn't wanted to believe it then, but now he was quite resigned to her betrayal. All the same, the memory still had the power to scrape across his senses, grating on his nerves, like a scar that wouldn't heal. He never had met the man in question. He had only known that he was some associate of Chris's, who had spent time at Nazeby, ostensibly recuperating from an illness. In those days, he had avoided Nazeby whenever possible, making excuses for his absence in the complicated demands of his work. He had seen his uncle often enough in London, and whenever Chris was in town, they had a meal together. But he hadn't wanted to see Isabel, in case the knowledge she and Chris were having problems overcame his resolution. He was still attracted to her, he had acknowledged that. And the fact that she was unhappy was a constant aggravation. But her defection with Jarrold Palmer had proved the ultimate deterrent. The man had done him a favour. By the time she appealed to him for help, he had had no feeling left for her.

But that was then, and this was now, he reminded himself grimly, entering Diana Laurence's office with a scowl on his face. And however distasteful the truth might seem to him, seeing Isabel again today had not convinced him of his immunity. In all honesty, he had hated himself for destroying her arguments, as he had done in the boardroom, and however justifiable his case had been, he had felt an utter bastard for making her look small. And she had looked small as she had gathered the documents she had brought together, and submitted to the will of the majority. But she hadn't avoided his eyes when the meeting was concluded, and the dignity he had seen in hers had torn him to the quick. That was why he had been so angry with Chris, and his uncle for that matter, when they had been gloating over their success. He had felt like the Judas goat, used to bait the trap; the treacherous pawn in his uncle's hands, sealing the fate of the queen.

'I gather the meeting did not go well,' murmured his secretary now, taking her cue from his expression, and Alex had to bite back the angry retort that sprang to his lips.

'As a matter of fact, the meeting was extremely successful,' he replied evenly, striding towards the door to his office. 'Are you going to lunch now, Diana? You can if you like. I shan't be needing you.'

'All right.' Diana pushed back her chair and stood up, but curiosity was getting the better of her, he could see it, and he was not surprised when she added a little appendage to her earlier remark. 'So—your uncle has got control of Mattley Pharmaceuticals, after all.'

'After all,' agreed Alex ironically, opening his door and giving her a mocking glance. 'Doesn't he always?' he remarked, rhetorically, and disappeared inside before she could take him up on it.

But although he could close his office door, he could not close his mind to thoughts of Isabel. Even after swallowing a rather stiff Scotch from the supply he kept in his office for the use of clients—something he never did at lunch time—he was still tormented by her image as he had last seen her. What was she thinking of him? he wondered. She probably despised him for doing Robert's job for him. She had always chided him for being his uncle's lackey, and this latest incident would only have strengthened her belief.

So why did he care? he asked himself, angrily, walking across to the windows and staring out at the sunlit streets below him. However pathetic she had seemed today, she was still the same Isabel who had led him on and then rejected him; cheated on her husband, and then appealed to him to take her part. She was completely without scruple, and if he wanted to keep his sanity, he should banish her from his thoughts.

The sound of the phone ringing behind him interrupted his mood. He waited for a moment, expecting Diana to answer it, and then, when she didn't, he recalled he had told her to go to lunch. Evidently, she had switched the line through to his office when she went out. Why else would it be ringing? he asked himself impatiently, realising that his attention had been totally distracted.

'Yes? Seton speaking,' he said curtly, picking up the receiver, and then knew a sudden craving that it might be Isabel.

But the light tones that answered him were nothing like hers, and although they were feminine, there was no similarity. 'Alex? Alex, darling, is that you? I thought you were going to ring me. Haven't you forgiven me yet?'

Alex's disappointment was instant, and acute, but

he managed to overcome the bitter disillusionment that gripped him. 'Penny,' he said, managing to infuse a trace of warmth into his voice. 'What a surprise! I expected you'd be out of the country.'

'I was,' she replied, the quickly disguised censure in her voice revealing her frustration. 'I just got back from Cairo last night, but you hadn't left a message with my answering service, and I was worried. We are going to see one another again, aren't we, Alex? You can't really intend that we go our separate ways.'

Alex took a deep breath. His initial inclination was to offer his apologies, and get off the phone as quickly as possible. He wasn't in the mood for Penny's recriminations, and getting involved with her again was not the most sensible thing to do.

But then, he anticipated the evening ahead, with nothing more demanding on his schedule than calling up some other female, with possibly less attraction for him than Penny had right now, and thought again. Maybe this was what he needed, he told himself grimly. A night spent in Penny's demanding company, and he would be fairly exhausted by the morning. One thing was sure, with her or without her, he was unlikely to get much sleep, and at least she cared for him, or said she did . . .

CHAPTER EIGHT

IT RAINED on Saturday morning and Isabel, standing in the bay window of her living-room, drinking her morning cup of coffee, wondered what the weather was like in Madrid. No doubt hot and sunny, she reflected gloomily. Certainly warmer than it was in London, and with the added bonus of being able to go swimming in the hotel pool. She guessed Lauren and Helen, and the other two girls who were on the assignment, were having a marvellous time. Lots of sun, the chance to wear beautiful clothes, and the happy awareness that they were being paid for it as well.

She sighed. Well, it was her own fault she wasn't with them. Jason had been furious when she insisted on staying in England. She knew he had been close to firing her when she refused to change her mind. But pragmatism, and perhaps his affection for her, had won the day, and eventually, he had agreed to her absence, albeit with bad grace.

And now she was wondering why she had bothered to risk her job, and her friendship with Jason, so that Alex could make a fool of her once again. The board meeting had been a fiasco, at least so far as she was concerned. All her fine schemes to thwart Robert Seton had come to nothing. From the minute Alex began delineating the reasons why Mattley Pharmaceuticals needed this merger with Denby Industries, Isabel had known she was fighting a losing battle. The smaller company was apparently in debt; it had gambled much of its resources on the research into a

new, and supposedly, miracle cure for arthritis, only
to have its development arrested by the findings of a
government agency, investigating drug abuse. One of
the ingredients of the capsule they were developing
had been found to be habit-forming, and all research
using Mirafen had been halted. The company needed
immediate financial assistance, or almost five hundred
employees, many of them research chemists, would
lose their jobs. Ally to this the fact that Denby was in
the market for a research laboratory, for its developing chemical industry, and Isabel was left with no
argument. Her own unqualified contention that the
smaller firm's independence was being undermined by
the proposed take-over simply wasn't credible, and
she forbore from voicing it. Instead, when the vote
was taken, she acquiesced, and had had to suffer the
ignominy of aiding in Robert Seton's undisguised
triumph.

It had been a sobering experience, finding herself
outflanked and outmanoeuvred, though she couldn't
in all honesty say that Alex had taken any satisfaction
in his victory. He had merely been stating the facts
and, surrounded by the other members of the board,
who had all supported the motion, she had been
unable to think of any reasonable objection.

But her defeat, if that was what it was, had left her
feeling totally deflated. Somehow, she had built herself
up for a confrontation that had never happened, and
now she had an awful feeling of anticlimax. She should
have gone with Jason, she reflected glumly. She should
have known that she would only be wasting her time
trying to balk Robert Seton. What chance did she
have against the might of a conglomerate? None at
all, even had her case been genuine. But it hadn't; and
she'd achieved absolutely nothing.

She turned away from the window dejectedly,
surveying the room behind her without satisfaction.

What was she going to do today? What *could* she do?
There was always housework, of course, but as she
paid a daily woman to come in twice a week to keep
the place tidy, there was nothing spoiling. She could
go out for a walk, although the rain seemed to put a
question mark on the advisability of that. So—what?
The hairdresser? *Shopping?* She pulled a wry face. She
had to eat, so probably that was the most sensible
suggestion. She would go up into the West End and
buy some pâté at Fortnum and Masons. She deserved
some compensation for giving up the trip to Madrid.
And, at least, she could afford it! The income which,
her solicitor had informed her, would be earned by
the shares she held in Denby Industries meant she
need never work again, if she didn't want to. She
could live in luxury for the rest of her life. Was that
what Vinnie had intended?

Thinking of Lady Denby brought her thoughts full
circle and, depositing her empty cup in the kitchen,
she went into her bedroom and flung herself on to the
unmade bed. 'What a tangled web you've left behind,
Vinnie,' she announced to the empty room, and then
rolled on to her stomach to rest her head on her
folded arms.

What had the old lady been thinking of, leaving the
shares to her? she wondered for the umpteenth time.
It wasn't as if Vinnie had nurtured any hopes that she
and Chris might get back together again. On the
contrary, his grandmother had helped her to leave
Nazeby and had supported her financially until she
could find a job and support herself. Of course, she
had paid the old lady back; every penny. But that still
didn't explain her generosity now.

Isabel sighed. The two years she had spent at
Nazeby would have been pretty bleak without Vinnie's
friendship. She had been the only real ally she had
had in that household, although it had taken her some

time to discover it. Robert Seton had never liked her.
He had never wanted her to marry Chris, and he had
made no secret of the fact. Chris himself she had
thought to be her friend, as well as her husband, but
he had ultimately betrayed her. And Alex . . .
Alex . . .

She swallowed. Her relationship with Chris's cousin
had never been a simple one. From the moment Alex
had come upon her and Chris in the library, he had
been an enigma to her. She never knew why he had
taken such an instinctive dislike to her, but he had,
and he had taken pains to avoid being in her company.
The fact that he had become a dominant force in her
life had troubled her a lot. She hadn't wanted to feel
so conscious of him whenever he was around, particularly when his own hostility towards her was so
acute. But in this her senses betrayed her, and right
from the start she had been aware of an unwilling
attraction towards him.

She had had no suspicion that he saw her as
anything more than an annoying intruder until the
afternoon he had given her a ride to Nazeby. And
even then, their initial conversation had given her no
clue to his real character. Oh, Chris had told her that
his cousin had had dozens of girlfriends, and that he
was immensely attractive to women, but in spite of
her own attraction to him, Isabel had seen no evidence
that Alex Seton possessed any more feelings than his
Uncle Robert. She had thought him a cold man, who
probably used women to satisfy his baser needs,
without ever becoming emotionally involved himself.
She had always found him distant and sarcastic, and
she had naturally assumed that he would never relax
with her.

And his manner at the start of that journey had
reinforced this opinion. He had been both distant and
mocking, though he had shown some compassion

when she had told him about her parentage. She didn't know why she had confided in him. In all honesty, she hadn't even told Chris the whole story and, with hindsight, it seemed the height of foolishness to have exposed her possible illegitimacy to Alex. But it was done and, so far as she knew, he had never betrayed her to his uncle.

But that was a small thing compared to what had happened after. And then it had been her objections to his rudeness that had precipitated the argument. And she had had justification, she reflected, remembering what he had said to her. But, even then, she had acted totally on impulse when she ran away from him.

If she had stopped to think, she would have realised how foolhardy she was being by taking off like that. If Alex had taken her at her word and driven off and left her, she dreaded to think what might have happened, and that nameless prospect had haunted her for many nights to come.

But at the time, she had not been thinking reasonably, and remembering how Alex had forced his way through a bramble hedge to follow her brought a smile to her lips even now. It was such an unusual sight: the immaculate Alexander Seton, with his hair all tangled, and threads of mohair hanging from his jacket. If she hadn't been in such a sorry state herself, she would have burst out laughing. But at least she had discovered he was human, that he had humour. She had glimpsed the man behind the mask, and when he smiled, her heart had skipped a beat.

He had been so nice about it, she recalled, rolling on to her back and gazing blankly up at the scrolled ceiling. He hadn't lost his temper, or been scathing, as she had naturally expected. He had actually thrown down his jacket, so that she could get out of the bog, and then cleaned her shoes up for her, so that no one would ever have guessed they had once been caked with mud.

But then, when they got back to the car, everything had gone wrong. Instead of capitalising on his good humour, she had made him impatient with her again. She hadn't realised he was so eager to get going until he reached past her to slam the door. Then, when she had sat up and trapped his arm, the outcome had been inevitable.

Or that was how it had seemed. When he had touched her, when the strong hard length of his fingers had closed about her breast, she had felt powerless to stop him. Oh, she had made some preliminary protest, trying to fight him when he pulled her into his arms, clamping her lips together in an effort to repulse him. But it had all been useless. She hadn't really wanted him to stop, and somehow he had known it, and when his mouth took possession of hers, she had responded with an urgency that frightened her. Chris had never made her feel like that; he had never kissed her like that, thrusting his hot tongue into her mouth, until she had almost swooned from the pleasure he was giving her.

But still, it wasn't enough. She had wanted more. She had wanted *him;* and the barrier presented by their clothes had seemed an insurmountable complication. She had known he wanted to make love to her, too. The feverish invasion of his hands had been just a sensual foretaste of how it could be between them, and when they had been disturbed, Isabel could have cried with frustration.

After that, nothing was the same any more. By the time the policeman had finished his inspection, Isabel had been made to feel like some cheap tramp, only worthy of jumping in the back of a car, and Alex had reverted to the cold, detached stranger she was used to dealing with.

She had had a bad moment, when they were on their way again, when she had wondered if what had happened had not been a deliberate set-up, devised by Robert Seton to prove to his son she was no better than she should be. But when she had asked Alex if he intended to tell Chris, he had denied it, and to her knowledge he never had.

But that weekend at Nazeby had been difficult for both of them. Until then, she had had no real doubts about her relationship with Chris, and attending the rehearsal of the wedding, she had realised it was a little late to have second thoughts. Besides, Chris had been so sweet to her in those days, and she had succeeded in convincing herself that what had happened with Alex had been a momentary aberration.

So confident was she that her feelings for Alex were purely sexual, that when he came to the flat where she was living, the night before the wedding, she had had no hesitation about turning him away. In any case, Alex himself had been drunk and abusive, and not until he tried to touch her was she in any danger of giving in to him.

But then, he had touched her, and she had been terrified that if he succeeded in kissing her, she would not be able to resist him. Once she was married, she had told herself desperately, she would not feel this weakness towards him; once she and Chris had consummated their relationship, she would no longer feel this shameful need for a man who clearly only wanted her as his mistress.

In those days, Chris's reticence about making love to her had seemed endearingly old-fashioned, and she had always felt that her own willingness to respect his wishes until after the wedding was perfectly natural.

That was why her attraction to his cousin was so contemptible, and as soon as Alex pulled her against

him and she felt the exciting thrust of his arousal, she
had acted purely on instinct. She had to get away
from him, she had to escape him, before the prospect
of surrendering to his naked passion became too
desirable to resist.

She had used the iron without thinking, never
dreaming that its weight would make up for any lack
of strength on her part. But when he let out that howl
of pain and staggered back against the door, she had
been almost frantic with horror, and if he had let her
tend him then, it might have been quite a different
story.

Of course, she had gone ahead with the wedding.
Pride was a strange bedfellow, and it was pride as
much as anything that got her to the altar. She had
no intention of letting Robert Seton think his disapproval had discouraged her, and besides, she wanted
to prove to Alex that she had chosen the better man.

Isabel shook her head now. How stupid she had
been! Just how stupid, she had learned on her wedding
night. By the time she and Chris came back from
honeymoon, she had been drawn and nervous, and
miserably aware that she had locked herself into a
marriage that was no marriage at all.

She had tried to end it as soon as they were back
in England. Unable to appeal to Chris, she had gone
to his father and begged him to let her have the
marriage annulled, but he had been incensed that she
should dare to bring such a problem to him. She was
lying, he said. Chris was perfectly normal; he was his
son; and no two-bit stripper was going to make his
son a laughing-stock.

He had threatened her, too, telling her that if she
tried to leave Nazeby, he would personally see to it
that she never worked again. And she believed him.
Robert Seton did not make empty threats. His
competitors in business had learned that often enough.

Chris used to delight in relating his father's exploits to her, but she had never dreamt that ruthless determination would ever be turned against her. She had been shocked, and frightened. She had only been eighteen, after all, and without any money of her own, she was helpless.

She considered calling his bluff and running away anyway, but somehow the opportunity never presented itself. Besides, the pride that had got her into this situation asserted itself sufficiently to enable her to try and make the marriage work. Chris was still Chris, after all, and in his way he still loved her. Or so she thought.

She had been weak; she had realised that afterwards. She had let Robert Seton manipulate her, without making any real fight for her independence. She had let the freedom from money worries, the beauty of her surroundings and her affection for Chris seduce her into a state of near-inertia, and only when she saw Alex did she feel like the coward she really was.

She had made excuses for herself, of course. Anyone who had been brought up in the austerity of a children's home could appreciate the luxury of having a room of her own, in what was undoubtedly one of the finest country houses in England. She had the chance to buy as many clothes as she liked, so long as she charged them to Chris's account, naturally; and the food that was served at Nazeby would make even a connoisseur's mouth water. Materially, she had everything she had ever wanted, and if the relationship between her and her father-in-law had never achieved its earlier tolerance, at least she had been able to put his threats to the furthest recesses of her mind.

And Vinnie had been there to smooth her passage. For some reason, Lady Denby had taken her under her wing, and although Isabel had never made the

mistake of confiding in her while she was married to
Chris, somehow the old lady had guessed that all was
not as it should be.

Looking back, those two years at Nazeby had
assumed a little of the substance of a dream. They
had never seemed entirely real, even when she was
living them, and she had learned exactly how unreal
her marriage was when she found Chris with Jerrold
Palmer.

She shivered, rolling on to her stomach again and
digging her nails into the bedspread. That, she
supposed, had been the worst moment of those two
years; worse even than the shock she had had when
she was served with divorce papers citing Jerrold
Palmer as *her* co-respondent.

Her immediate thought had been, how had Robert
Seton persuaded Palmer to participate in such a decep-
tion? But, the answer had been equally as swiftly
supplied. Evidently, Jerrold Palmer had as little desire
as Chris to have his sexual aberrations aired in public,
and their joint testimony against her was totally
damning.

Oh, she had been staggered that Chris's father
should sink to such depths to protect his son, but she
should have known that where his family's name was
concerned, Robert Seton was implacable. *If there's no
defence, attack!* she had read somewhere, and Robert
Seton certainly used this as his motto. She was to be
sacrificed, and from Robert Seton's point of view, he
was accomplishing a dual achievement. Chris would
emerge as an innocent bystander, while anything she
said would be negated by her presumed bitterness at
being found out. He had wanted rid of her long
enough, goodness knows. Only the fear of what she
might betray had forced him to keep her at Nazeby.

Of course, she had appealed to Chris to change his
mind, begging him to tell the truth and exonerate her.

He could have a divorce, she said. The marriage could be annulled any time he wanted it. He had only to say the word.

But Chris had refused to speak to her. She guessed his father had given him his instructions, and a week after the papers were served, he had taken himself off to the continent, leaving her no forwarding address, and effectively abandoning her to her fate. Even Vinnie wasn't there to help her. She was in Australia, visiting an old friend in Melbourne, whose address again Isabel did not know. Besides, events were moving so swiftly, by the time she got back to England, it would be much too late for her to do anything.

Which left only one person she could turn to—Alex. He was the only person she knew with sufficient influence—and resources—to plead her case. She had little money of her own. She had never liked to ask Chris for any, and as most of her needs had been satisfied by a credit card, she had used her small savings to cover any personal expenses. Only now did she realise how advantageous her position was to Robert Seton. Without money she was helpless, and he must have known it.

For days after the idea of approaching Alex had come into her mind, she had thought of little else. Pacing the empty rooms at Nazeby, she had persuaded herself that if he knew the truth, he would be sympathetic. She had always loved Nazeby, but during those long, anxious days, she had grown to hate it, realising Robert had left her there to appreciate how powerless she was against the might of the Seton organisation.

Nevertheless, the notion to contact Alex took root, and with it, the realisation that a doctor's examination might disprove Chris's lies. Surely if she told Alex the truth, he would help her. Even after all that had happened between them, she trusted him. He was his uncle's protégé, that was true, but he had always had a mind of his own.

She went up to London the next day, driving the Audi estate car, which had always been at her disposal. No one tried to stop her. Robert Seton had given her six weeks to find somewhere else to live, and she guessed the staff at Nazeby imagined she was house-hunting.

She had never been to the apartment Alex occupied at that time, but she knew it was in a tower block near Hyde Park, which wasn't hard to find. She had chosen to come on a Saturday morning, in the hope that she might find him at home. The idea of approaching him at his office had seemed too formal. Besides, she had had no wish for any member of his staff to feel obliged to report her visit to his uncle.

She had left Nazeby early, and it was barely nine-thirty when she pushed through the smoked-glass doors of Romsey Court. She knew, from what Chris had told her, that Alex's apartment was on the fifteenth floor, but what she had not bargained for was the fact that the building was patrolled by a highly efficient security staff.

A man in a grey uniform vetted all visitors to the apartments from a steel and plate-glass desk, set to one side of the foyer, and Isabel felt like an intruder as his features took on an inquiring expression.

'Um—I'd like to go up to Mr Seton's apartment,' she explained, approaching the desk as he rose to his feet to face her. 'Mr *Alex* Seton. At 1504.'

The man studied her intently for a moment, and then inclined his head. 'Very well,' he said, indicating the lifts. 'Go ahead. I'll inform Mr Seton's butler that a visitor is on her way up.'

'Thank you.'

Isabel supposed it could have been worse. The man could have asked her name, and she was not at all convinced that under those circumstances, Alex would have agreed to see her. Instead, the officer had apparently decided she was harmless. Either that, or Alex's butler was a force to be reckoned with.

The diminutive Irishman who opened the door of Alex's apartment at her ring was neither huge nor intimidating. But he was evidently surprised to see her, and once again Isabel was obliged to state her business.

'I—er—I'd like to see Alex,' she said, unquestionably daunted by another unfriendly face. If she'd known how difficult it was going to be to see him, she probably wouldn't have come.

'And is Mr Seton expecting you, miss?' enquired the man, with the smug air of one who already knows the answer to his question, and Isabel sighed.

'It's *Mrs*, actually,' she said. 'Mrs *Seton!* And no, he's not expecting me, but I think he'll see me all the same.'

It was amusing to watch his dawning comprehension, or it would have been if Isabel had felt less tense. As it was, she waited impatiently for some recognition, wishing deep inside her there had been some other way.

'Would that be Mrs—*Christopher* Seton?' the Irishman appended, after a moment, his brogue thickening as his thoughts occupied themselves with this new development.

'Just—Mrs Seton will do,' Isabel averred flatly, glancing beyond him into a living-room that seemed filled with light. 'May I come in? I gather Alex is at home.'

Kerry O'Flynn, as she later learned his name to be, stepped back abruptly. 'Sure, why not?' he agreed, clearly too uncertain of her relationship with his employer to keep her standing there while he went to inform his master of her arrival. 'Come forward, won't you? I'll let Mr Seton know you're here. I think he's awake. I took him his breakfast quite a while ago.'

'He's still in bed?' exclaimed Isabel, stepping inside on to a polished wood-blocked floor, and the Irishman nodded as he closed the door behind her.

'Ah, the man was working half the night, wasn't he?' he declared, without really requiring a reply. 'Now, if you'll wait here, Mrs Seton, I'll see what's going on.'

Isabel saw immediately why the huge living-room of the apartment seemed so bright. Because the apartment was on the corner of the building, two walls of plate-glass windows gave an uninterrupted view of the park nearby. Reinforced double glazing cut out all intrusive sounds from the street below, and the long, slanting blinds could be turned to take advantage of the light.

The room itself was just as luxurious as she had expected, although the colour scheme was surprisingly subdued. A thick Oriental rug occupied most of the floor space, while two enormous sofas faced one another across the width of a lacquered coffee-table. A modern desk, with a tubular, cushioned chair beside it, was set beneath one of the windows, and the walls were hung with groups of etchings, mostly Oriental again in design. It was a comfortable, uncluttered room, with the minimum amount of ornamentation. Yet there were some attractive pieces adorning the stereo unit and the bookshelves, solid carvings of jade and crystal, that blended well with the other appointments.

Isabel was admiring a cut-glass figurine when she became aware that she was no longer alone. She turned, half expecting to find the butler, ready to make his apologies, and instead found Alex, dark and intensely disturbing, and evidently not pleased to see her. In a knee-length navy blue bathrobe and little else, he looked grim and unapproachable, and Isabel, who hadn't seen him in months, felt a treacherous surge of emotion.

'Oh—Alex!' she said, moistening her lips and setting the figurine she was holding back on its shelf. 'Er—thank you for seeing me.'

'I don't have much choice, as you're here!' he remarked, without expression. 'What do you want, Isabel? Chris is not here. And I don't have his address, if that's what you're thinking.'

Isabel took a deep breath. 'I didn't come here to ask where Chris was.' She paused to control the tremor in her voice, and then went on, 'Believe it or not, I don't care where he is; or who he's with, for that matter. I—I came to see you. I should have done so long ago.'

Alex's dark brows descended. 'Really?'

'Yes, really.' Isabel took a step towards him. 'Oh, Alex, why did you let me marry Chris? Why didn't you stop me, when you had the chance?'

'When *I* had the chance?' Alex's brows arched now in apparent disbelief. 'Isabel, your reasons for marrying my cousin were nothing to do with me. And I couldn't have stopped you. I wouldn't have wanted to.'

'That's not true!' Isabel bit her lips frustratedly.

'I assure you——'

'Oh, for once in your life, be honest, can't you?' she cried. 'You *could* have stopped me. You know it, and I know it. But we both behaved stupidly, and now—and now I'm paying the price!'

Alex gave her a scathing look. 'I understood it was Chris who was paying the price, as you put it,' he remarked bleakly. 'I hope you're not trying to blame me for this—affair you've been having with Jerrold Palmer——'

'I haven't been having an affair with Jerrold Palmer!' Isabel interrupted him desperately. 'Alex—that was

Chris! Not me! Your uncle devised the whole thing. To frame me, and to protect his precious son!'

Alex stared at her scornfully. 'You mean, Chris made the whole thing up?' He shook his head. 'I don't believe it!'

'No, that's not what I meant——'

'So, he didn't make it up?'

'No! That is—Alex, you don't understand!'

'Well, that's the truest thing you've said since you got here,' he agreed harshly. 'I think you'd better go, Isabel. You and I have nothing to say to one another.'

Isabel moved her head from side to side, unwilling and unable to believe that Alex wouldn't even listen to her. 'Please,' she begged. 'You've got to believe me. I haven't done anything!'

'You're wasting your time, Isabel.' Alex's mouth had hardened. 'You forget—I know you! I know what an unscrupulous creature you are. Anyone who could behave as you did on the eve of her wedding——'

'That wasn't my fault!'

'Then whose fault was it?'

'You came to where I lived, Alex!'

'Because I'd found out what you were really like, and would have done anything to protect Chris——'

'No!'

'Yes.' He was inflexible. 'My God! And you had the audacity to come to me to get you out of this mess you've got yourself into. I don't know how you had the nerve——'

'Alex——'

'—Just because I didn't tell Chris what a randy little bitch you were first time around is no reason for you to believe I'd defend you now. Christ, I don't know how he's put up with you for so long. I saw through you, right from the start. And if one man wasn't enough for you you should have had the decency to get out, instead of making a fool of Chris with one of his own friends!'

Isabel flung herself at him then. A combination of pain and anguish and bitter disappointment had balled in her stomach, and she needed to expunge at least a bit of it or go out of her mind.

'You—you brute!' she sobbed, all thought of explaining how a doctor's testimony might clear her name going out of her head. All she could think was that Alex was her enemy, and that, far from supporting her innocence, he actually believed what Chris had told him.

Alex was unprepared for her initial attack, and her nails raked his chest in the opened 'V' of his bathrobe, and her knee almost made contact with that most vulnerable part of his anatomy before he was able to control her. But quick reflexes, and a superior strength, rapidly quelled the effectiveness of her assault, and Isabel was reduced to swearing at him as his hands imprisoned hers at her sides.

'Bastard!' she mumbled impotently, as the fight went out of her and, as hot tears overspilled her eyes, Alex stifled an expletive and released her.

'I think you'd better go.'

Isabel turned away, drawing a hand across her eyes as she did so. She couldn't bear to look at him, not just then, and the knowledge that he despised her, too, was the final humiliation.

She never remembered how she got back to Nazeby. She must have driven there, because the Audi was back in the garage the next morning, when she loaded her few belongings into it. She took only those things she had brought to Nazeby. All the expensive suits and dresses she had bought since her marriage to Chris, she left hanging in the wardrobes.

After making arrangements for the car's return with the housekeeper, she drove away from Nazeby for the last time. A week later, she found a room in a house in Bayswater, and an allowance from the social services tided her over until she found a job.

And there she stayed until Lady Denby returned from Australia and discovered what had happened in her absence. Of course, the old lady had come to see her, and in spite of Isabel's reluctance to accept anything from the family, she had insisted on finding her a small flat. The two-roomed apartment in Earl's Court was not exactly what Lady Denby had wanted her to have, but Isabel had insisted it was all she was going to be able to afford, and Vinnie had respected her wishes.

Isabel sighed now. Chris's grandmother had never asked any questions. She had never mentioned Chris's name in connection with the divorce, or queried Isabel's association with Jerrold Palmer. She had allowed Isabel to tell her, only if *she* wanted, and it was many months before Isabel had confessed that she had not been the guilty party.

Even then, she remembered, she had been wary of making any claims against her ex-husband. After the way his father and his cousin had reacted, she had been half afraid his grandmother wouldn't believe her story either. But Vinnie had made no judgement either way, and when the whole truth was revealed, she had merely put her arms around Isabel and comforted her in the only way she knew how. It wasn't until Vinnie's solicitors had contacted her after her death that Isabel had appreciated the full extent of Lady Denby's faith in her, and the gift of the shares now seemed the final exculpation. Was that why she needed so desperately to hang on to them? Because they represented the fact that someone had believed in her?

CHAPTER NINE

ISABEL was folding the hems of soft, tan leather pants into fringed cream boots when the intercom buzzed. Frowning, she finished putting on the second boot, and then went to lift the receiver. She couldn't imagine who it might be, unless Jason had cut short his trip to Spain. But, remembering how angry he had been with her before he went away, she didn't think that was likely.

'Yes?'

'Isabel?'

It was Alex's voice, and her stomach gave a sickening little lurch. *Alex?* What did he want? After her painful reminiscences earlier, he was the last person she wanted to see.

Swallowing, she kept her voice as expressionless as possible, 'Yes. What do you want, Alex?'

'Can I come up?'

Isabel almost gasped. 'I don't think that's a very good idea,' she replied distantly. 'If it's something to do with the shares, I suggest you contact my solicitor——'

'It's nothing to do with the shares,' he interrupted her harshly. 'I want to talk to you. Preferably not standing in the pouring rain.'

Isabel hesitated. 'If it's about the board meeting——'

'I've told you, it's nothing to do with Denby's!' He sighed. 'Please.'

Isabel's lips parted. Alex, saying *please!* Now that was really something. Besides, she was curious to know what had brought him here on a *Saturday*

139

morning. It seemed out of character, somehow.

'I—all right,' she said at last, coming to a decision. She pressed a button. 'Push the door. It's open.'

She had unlocked her door by the time he had climbed the stairs, leaving it ajar so that she could take up a position in the window bay. With the light behind her, she had a momentary advantage, although, as it was such a dull day, the advantage was very small.

Alex reached the door and opened it tentatively. Then, glimpsing her across the room, he stepped inside and closed the door behind him. The brief time it took him to secure the latch gave Isabel a chance to look at him unobserved, and in spite of her determination to be cool and detached, it was still unnerving to have him there.

He had evidently had to walk after leaving his car, and his dark hair was damp and moulded to his scalp. Its wetness accentuated the fact that he needed a haircut, and where it brushed his collar, it curled upwards with irrepressible vitality. He was wearing black trousers and a matching black suede jerkin, both of which were smudged with water, but it was his lean face that held her attention, and the disturbingly black eyes that he now turned in her direction.

'Isabel,' he acknowledged, by way of a greeting, unzipping his jacket and shaking drops of rain-water from his wrists. 'What a morning!'

'Miserable, isn't it?' Isabel took her cue from him. 'I was just about to go shopping, but I'm not looking forward to it.'

'I wouldn't if I were you,' Alex put in wryly. 'The West End is clogged with traffic, and you can't find a parking-space to save your life.'

Isabel shrugged. 'I was going to take a taxi.'

'Ah.' Alex nodded. 'And is it essential?'

'The shopping?' And after gaining his acquiescence, 'I have to eat.'

Alex inclined his head. 'I see.' Then, startling her, he added, 'You could eat with me.'

'With you?' The words were out before she could prevent them, and she saw his instinctive withdrawal at her incredulous words.

'Even bastards eat,' he remarked drily, and to her surprise she saw a hint of colour invading his cheeks.

'I—well——' His behaviour had disconcerted her. Whatever reason he had had for coming here, she would never have believed it was to invite her for a *meal!* 'I don't know what to say.'

Alex shrugged now and, noticing that the trickling dampness from his hair was invading his neck, Isabel crossed the room to her bedroom, emerging a few moments later with an apricot-coloured hand-towel. 'Here,' she said, handing it to him. 'You'd better take off your coat.'

'Thanks.' Alex did as he was bidden, and Isabel dragged her eyes away from the evidence of taut muscle silhouetted beneath the silk of his pale blue shirt. As he towelled his hair dry, she cupped her elbows in her hands and turned to face the rain-swept view of the park outside. Anything rather than look at him, she thought tensely. She had been a fool to think she still hated him. If she ever had, it was long ago now. Although she might deny it, her feelings came from a vastly different source.

'Well?'

He spoke again then and, swinging round to face him, Isabel found he had put his jacket on again. However, with his hair ruffled by its towelling and his eyelashes still glinting with a few errant drops of rain-water, he was distractingly approachable. Too approachable, she acknowledged tautly. She was used

to seeing his public face; his private one was much
too human.

Swallowing, she assumed an expression of smiling
inconsequence. 'I—can't believe you came here on a
wet Saturday morning, just to invite me out to lunch,'
she declared lightly, relieved to find she sounded
infinitely more confident that she felt. If he knew how
the thought of having lunch with him was chewing
her up, he wouldn't doubt that sooner or later he'd
persuade her to sell the shares.

'I didn't,' he said now, in answer to her remark,
and she kept the smile glued to her face by an immense
effort of will. She should have known, she thought
bitterly. Every day was a working day to someone like
Alex Seton. He would use any means that were necessary to get into her apartment, but once he was there,
he had no reason to sustain the act.

Swallowing again, she bit back her disappointment.
'Well, then, I suggest——' she began harshly, but he
interrupted her before she could finish.

'I came to apologise,' he said, astounding her
completely. 'What I did on Thursday morning
was—unprofessional. I should have had the relevant
papers delivered to you in advance of the meeting, so
that you could have been prepared for what was said.
But instead, I took Robert's line, and put you on the
spot. There's no excuse for it, but I wanted you to
know I've felt bloody bad about it ever since!'

Isabel was glad the window was behind her, as her
hands sought the sill for support. She had thought she
had heard everything when he asked to be allowed to
come up. But this—this was totally out of character,
and her brain worked desperately, trying to ascertain
some reason for his apparent change of heart.

'So,' he said at last, 'the least I can do is offer to
buy you lunch. Will you accept?'

Isabel made a helpless gesture. 'Did your uncle send you here——'

'No.'

'This isn't some new ploy to gain my confidence or something?'

'No.' Alex's denial was adamant. 'Believe it or not, but coming here was all my own idea. My uncle wouldn't approve, I can assure you.'

Isabel could believe it. She imagined Robert Seton would likely blow his top if he discovered his favourite nephew had been fraternising with the 'enemy'.

Now, she shook her head. 'Well, I—I'm grateful for your honesty, and—and I appreciate your taking the trouble to come here and tell me how you feel. But—there's really no need to take me to lunch——'

Alex's lips thinned. 'No *need*,' he agreed flatly. 'But it's what I'd like to do, anyway.'

Isabel licked her lips. 'Why?'

'I've told you.'

'To make amends?'

'Yes.'

'And I've told you there's no need.' She gathered all her composure and faced him squarely. 'I wouldn't like to put you out.'

The dark eyes were intense. 'And if it's what I want?'

Isabel caught her breath. 'I find that hard to believe.'

'Do you?' He breathed evenly. 'Well—that's still no reason for you to refuse me.'

Isabel shifted awkwardly. 'Alex——'

'Isabel?'

She pressed her lips together. 'You don't even like me!' she protested.

'I don't like myself much either,' he commented drily. 'But the fact remains, we both have to eat, and I see no real reason why we shouldn't do it together. Do you?'

Isabel could think of several, not least her own unwilling attraction towards him, that was being strained to its limits by his proximity. But still, she reflected weakly, there was probably less danger in having lunch with him in some restaurant than in arguing with him in the intimacy of her living-room. And she had already had one example of how that could end.

'All right,' she agreed at last, inwardly despising herself for her weakness. 'I'll have lunch with you. But afterwards——'

'Let's take one step at a time, shall we?' he suggested, the faintest suggestion of a frown marring his dark good looks. 'OK. Shall we go?'

Isabel hesitated. The flat-heeled boots and leather trousers had seemed suitable attire for tramping round the shops, but they were less appropriate for the kind of restaurant Alex probably patronised. Her hair, too, plaited into a braid that fell just below her shoulders, had been secured for convenience, rather than style, and only the cream silk shirt seemed acceptable.

'You look fine to me,' Alex inserted suddenly, and she realised he had guessed what she was thinking. 'Go on. Put on a coat or something. Just to keep your shoulders dry.'

In fact, Isabel paused long enough to apply a touch of mascara to her lashes, and a beige eyeshadow to her lids. With her exotic colouring, she needed little make-up, and the result was pleasing even to herself.

'I'm ready,' she said, emerging from her bedroom to find Alex occupying the position she had occupied earlier. Tying the belt of her dark green raincoat about her waist, she looked at him almost shyly, realising as he walked towards the door that this was the first time he had actually invited her company.

The Ferrari was parked a few yards along the street and, bidding Isabel wait under cover of the porch,

Alex sprinted towards it. Within seconds, he had unlocked the doors and climbed inside, starting the engine almost instantly, and reversing back to where she was waiting.

Isabel left her sanctuary as he pushed open the nearside door and, as she coiled herself into the seat beside him, she was uncomfortably reminded of the last time they had driven together.

'All right?' he asked, his eyes softer now, and distractingly gentle. She had never known Alex to be gentle, and the experience was unnerving. Oh, God, she thought, clamping her lips together, on no account must she make a fool of herself again!

As he had said, the roads were all jammed with traffic, everyone reverting to personal transport to avoid the discomfort of waiting for buses in the rain. Trying to drive into central London was a nightmare, but after realising that Alex had the situation under control, she sat back to enjoy the experience of driving in a car that attracted all eyes, even in the rain.

'An English summer,' she murmured ruefully, as they ground to a halt once again. 'I should have gone to Spain, after all.'

'Spain?' Alex glanced her way.

'Madrid, actually,' she conceded. 'I was supposed to be part of a shoot Jason's doing there.'

Alex frowned. 'So why aren't you?'

Isabel grimaced. 'Would you believe—the board meeting?'

There was silence for a while, and then Alex said incredulously, 'You gave up a trip to Spain to attend the board meeting?'

'That's right.' She shrugged. 'Stupid, wasn't it? Jason was really mad!'

Alex negotiated the next set of traffic lights, and then said tersely, 'You and Ferry—you spend a lot of time together?'

Isabel looked his way. 'Some,' she admitted cautiously. 'We're—friends. He's been very kind to me. I owe him a lot.'

'How much?'

It was an odd question, but Isabel took it at its face value. 'He took a chance and employed me, when no one else would,' she replied evenly. 'The agency I worked for before I—before I was married, wouldn't even consider me. They prefer—younger models. Not mid-twenties divorcees, who've forgotten how to move their bodies.'

Alex made a curious sound. 'Do you forget?'

'Oh, yes.' Isabel was serious. 'A good model is the result of good training. You can't walk in off the street and do it.'

Alex's glance was faintly mocking. 'It's a profession, then?'

'As I once told you,' she reminded him swiftly, and then relaxed. He wasn't baiting her today. He was being incredibly nice, as a matter of fact. Too nice, she warned herself fiercely. What was it they said about the smile on the face of the tiger?

It wasn't until they were crossing the Hammersmith Bridge that Isabel realised they were not going into the West End after all. Until then, she had been prepared to concede the fact that Alex probably knew his way around London better than she did. Besides, the rain made aliens of the most familiar sights, and only the river remained the same, whatever the state of the weather.

'Where are we going?' she asked, her voice not quite as sharp as it might have been had she not suspected he was taking her to some surburban road-house. 'We seem to be leaving the city behind.'

'We are.' Alex cast her a reassuring look. 'So, tell me, what would you be doing now, if you were in Madrid?'

Isabel bit her lip. The temptation to demand an answer to her question was compelling, but she didn't want to spoil their tenuous harmony. 'Oh—working, I suppose,' she conceded, lifting her shoulders in a careless gesture. 'I'd probably be too hot, but I'd be looking forward to a swim later. That's one of the advantages of staying at an hotel. They always have a pool, and we—that is, the other girls and I—usually take full advantage of it.'

'And Ferry?' inserted Alex softly. 'Does he join you?'

Isabel hesitated. 'Sometimes.'

'Most times?'

'Just—sometimes,' she said, turning to look out of the window. 'Where are we?'

'Are you in love with him?' Alex asked beside her, and his words brought her round to face him.

'No!'

'Are you sure?'

'Of course I'm sure.' She felt the hot colour invade her cheeks none the less. 'In any case, that's my business. Isn't it?'

Alex shrugged. 'What time is it?' he asked then, changing the subject completely, and she fumed.

'It's a quarter past twelve,' she said, glancing at her watch automatically, before staring rather ostentatiously at the clock on the console. 'Isn't it?'

'So it is.' His lips twitched. 'We should be there in time for a late meal, anyway.'

The interchange with the M3 was looming, and Isabel felt a sudden hollowing of her stomach. This was the way to Nazeby, she realised sickly. Oh, God, he must be taking her to see his uncle! And she had believed him when he said he wanted to apologise.

'Stop the car,' she said abruptly, gripping the strap of her shoulder-bag and mentally cursing herself for being so gullible. Why was she always so weak where

Alex was concerned? She already knew the answer, but that didn't make it any less unpalatable.

The Ferrari didn't slow its pace however, and she was not so foolish as to attempt to open the door at speed. She was no stuntwoman; her appearance earned her her living. If she leapt out now and broke a limb, her career would be in tatters.

'Alex, please,' she said, despising herself for begging him, but totally incapable of facing the prospect of meeting Robert Seton again on his own ground. 'Don't do this to me!' she pleaded, torturing the strap of her bag, and he shook his head impatiently as they ran down on to the motorway.

'Where do you think I'm taking you?' he asked, as the Ferrari picked up even more speed, and Isabel slumped in her seat.

'Nazeby,' she said dully, wondering why she didn't hate him now, when she had every reason for doing so. 'I'm right, aren't I? That is where we're headed. God, why did I believe you, when you said you wanted to apologise!'

Alex's lips twisted. ' "Oh, ye of little faith"!' he quoted wryly, settling more comfortably in his seat. 'Why do you think I'm taking you to Nazeby? So that Uncle Robert can capitalise on his victory?'

Isabel sniffed. 'Something like that. What does it matter? Anyway, I shan't get out of the car; so you'll have to bring me back.'

Alex made an amused sound. 'And if I tell you we have the place to ourselves? That Uncle Robert is in South America, and apart from Mrs Cowie and the other servants, the place is unoccupied. What then?'

Isabel gasped. 'You're not serious!'

'Why not?'

'Because—because—well, why there?'

Alex shrugged. 'To erase a bad memory, perhaps,' he remarked softly. 'Nazeby's not so bad; it's just the people in it. And,' his lips parted to reveal a lazy smile, 'there's always the pool. As I remember, you used to use it more than any of us.'

Isabel stared at him. 'How did you know that?'

'I used to watch you, on those rare occasions I was compelled to spend some time at the house. You know the partition that adjoins the conservatory is made of one-way glass? I could see you, but you couldn't see me.'

Isabel blinked. 'But why would you want to—watch me?'

'Voyeurism, what else?' he retorted, suddenly brusque. 'Look, it's a bit late now, but you will come, won't you? I phoned Mrs Cowie while you were getting ready, and she's expecting us.'

It was still raining when they reached the gates that gave access to the Denby estate, but not so heavily now. Instead, a drifting mist wreathed itself around the trunks of the trees in the park, rising from the earth that was still warm from the previous days of sun.

Nazeby itself nestled in its fold of the downs, lush now with the promise of high summer. There were foals in the paddocks that ran down to the river, and an abundance of blossom in the hedges that marked the boundary of the gardens.

Mrs Cowie, the housekeeper, opened the door as the Ferrari crunched to a halt on the gravelled fore-court. If she was surprised—or even shocked—to see the ex-wife of the son of the house, who had left here under a cloud, with her employer's nephew, she was too polite to show it. Instead, she offered a suitable greeting before excusing herself about her duties, and Alex led Isabel into the hall with obvious satisfaction.

'Why are you doing this?' she asked, in a low voice,

as they stood together in the panelled entrance hall, and Alex smiled.

'Why don't you take off your coat and freshen up?' he suggested, instead of giving her a reply. 'You know where everything is, so make yourself at home. I'm going to change these clothes. They feel decidedly damp.'

Isabel caught her lower lip between her teeth, still barely convinced that they were alone. But when he went ahead of her, up the curving arc of the carpeted staircase, to stand looking down at her from the galleried landing, she eventually subdued her fears and followed him, shivering at the memories the simple act evoked.

'Use this room,' Alex said, opening a door along one of the carpeted corridors, which ran in either direction from the head of the stairs, and reluctantly, Isabel stepped inside. It was one of the guest rooms, an attractive apartment, hung with ivory silk and cream damask; it was the room she had used in those traumatic days before she left Nazeby. And as such, no threat to her troubled sensitivities.

'I won't be long,' he added, as she walked slowly across the carpet, to stand gazing absently from the windows. 'Take off your coat. It's warm enough in here.'

But when he came back, Isabel was still standing by the window, and he came across the room towards her, dark and disturbing, in a lime-green polo shirt, and cotton shorts. 'No point in getting dressed, if we're going swimming,' he remarked, as her eyes widened. 'Don't worry. We'll find a bathing-suit for you. There's quite a selection in one of the changing-rooms downstairs. Uncle Robert always thinks of everything when he entertains guests.'

'Yes.'

Isabel's response was mildly ironic, and Alex

grimaced. 'OK, OK, I won't mention his name again. Now,' he took hold of the belt at her waist and tugged it loose, 'are you going to relax?'

Isabel's breathing had quickened at this unexpected, and decidedly proprietory, display of familiarity. She was not used to Alex touching her, not any part of her, and the brush of his fingers against her waist was much too close for comfort.

'I—I want to wash my hands,' she said abruptly, slipping off the coat, and dropping it on the floor. 'I'll—I'll see you downstairs. Just give me a few minutes.'

'As you wish.' Alex bent and picked up her coat and deposited it on the bed. 'I'll be waiting in the conservatory. I thought we could eat there, and anticipate our swim.'

Although Isabel washed her hands twice, they were still sweating when she went downstairs again. She told herself it was being in this house again, with all its hateful memories, but it wasn't true. Nazeby had always soothed her spirit, even in those terrible weeks following her discovery of Chris and Jerrold Palmer in the stables. It was only at the end that she had come to hate it. But that was because it had symbolised her helplessness. With hindsight, she could see that the house had not been to blame.

The conservatory adjoined the morning-room, and at this time of year, it was like an indoor garden. Hanging baskets, spilling over with fuchsias and geraniums, were suspended from every beam, while tubs and troughs of every kind of flowering blossom rioted in vivid colour across the Italian tiles.

Mrs Cowie had prepared them a cold buffet, and this occupied a side-table. A mosaic of meats and salads was artistically arranged around a whole dressed lobster, with dishes of fruit and cream to complete the meal. A circular glass-topped table had been laid for

two, and beside it, a chilled bottle of hock rested in
an ice bucket. It was a display made to fit its surroundings, and Isabel, who had forgotten how cosseted life
could be, pressed a nervous hand to her throat. It was
all too disturbingly familiar—and yet, not familiar at
all.

The solarium adjoined the conservatory. Sliding
glass screens could be rolled back to open up the
whole area, and the pool itself could be either outdoor
or indoor, according to the weather. At present, the
screens between the pool-house and the conservatory
were rolled back but, because of the weather, the pool
itself was enclosed by glass walls. There was something
rather satisfying about being able to swim whatever
the temperature was outside, and Isabel remembered
how much she had missed the privilege when she was
dogging the agencies, looking for work.

As she hovered by the table in the conservatory,
Alex emerged from one of the dressing-rooms that
adjoined the pool, and when he saw her, he grinned.
'I was just checking that we had a swimsuit to fit you,'
he called, circling the pool and climbing the two stone
steps that led into the conservatory. 'Do you want to
swim now, or later?'

Isabel moistened her lips. 'Oh—later, I think,' she
ventured awkwardly, daunted by the prospect of taking
off her clothes in front of Alex. Her skin was so pale
compared to the darkness of his, the long, powerful
legs exposed by his shorts revealing he did not spend
all his time in his office. Besides, he had never seen
her in a swimsuit before—with her knowledge, that is.
Those occasions when he said he had watched her
swimming didn't count. She had been unaware of his
observation.

'OK,' Alex agreed now, and picking up the bottle
of wine, he filled their two glasses. 'Here,' he said,
handing one of the delicate flutes to her. 'To better

times, hmm? Drink it. I think you'll like it.

Isabel did as she was told, the chilled mouthful she took spreading deliciously over her palate. 'It's lovely,' she said, in answer to his look of enquiry. 'This is lovely,' she added, using the colourful buffet to drag her eyes from his. 'Mrs Cowie has gone to a lot of trouble. Did—did she know who you were bringing?'

Alex took another taste of his wine, and then inclined his head. 'Yes, she knew. And no, she didn't make any comment,' he appended lazily. 'I don't need anyone's approval to bring you here. This is my home, too. I invite who I like.'

Isabel looked down into her glass. 'And if your uncle had been here?' she queried, and he gave her a wry smile.

'*You* wouldn't have come,' he replied, setting his glass down on the table. 'At least, only on sufferance. But if you had been willing, I dare say he'd have survived.'

Isabel sighed. 'Alex——'

'Why don't we eat?' he suggested, taking her glass from her and turning her towards the buffet table. 'Help yourself to anything you like. Mrs Cowie will only grumble if we don't do her efforts justice.'

CHAPTER TEN

In all honesty, Isabel wasn't very hungry. Her appetite had always been dependent upon her disposition and, in spite of Alex's efforts to relax her, she was still extremely tense. Even the careless touch of his hand at her elbow set her nerves jumping, and it was difficult to behave casually when she was so aware of him.

Two glasses of wine later, she felt much better. She had eaten some of the wafer-thin Italian ham with a slice of melon, and gorged herself on a plate of raspberries and whipped cream, even laughing when Alex wiped a smear of cream from her lip with his finger and then licked it. She felt relaxed and absurdly happy, and only when one of the maids came to clear and recognised her did she remember where she was and what she was doing.

'Alex,' she probed softly, when the maid had departed again with their dirty plates. 'Why? Why here? You know your uncle won't approve, whatever you say to the contrary.'

'I think we should take a sauna,' said Alex, without answering her, pushing back his chair and getting to his feet. 'I turned on the heater earlier, so it should be pretty hot by now.'

Isabel looked up at him and shook her head. 'A sauna!' she echoed. 'Straight after your meal!'

'No better way to cleanse your body of all that alcohol,' he responded, grinning. 'Aren't you going to join me? There's plenty of room.'

Isabel shook her head. 'I don't think so.'

'Why not?'

'Well . . . ' She moved her shoulders. 'It's too humid already.'

'OK. We'll swim then,' he declared easily. 'The water's fairly cool. Now, don't tell me you need time to digest your lunch. You didn't eat enough to warrant the effort.'

Isabel bit her lip. 'All right. If that's what you want.'

'I thought it was what you wanted,' Alex reminded her drily. 'I seem to remember something about a hotel pool . . . '

Isabel sighed. 'All right. All right.' She got to her feet. 'Which dressing-room should I use?'

'Whichever you like,' he replied carelessly. 'I left the swimsuits in the first one, but as I don't need one, you can choose another if you like.'

Isabel grimaced. 'Why should I do that?'

'I don't know.' Alex gave her a considering look. 'You might think I had an ulterior motive for that, too. Perhaps I've got a peep-hole in the wall of that changing-room, hmm?'

Isabel had to smile at that. 'I won't be long,' she said and, leaving him, she crossed the room and descended the few steps into the pool area.

The pool itself was just short of Olympic size, with diving-boards and a water-slide, as well as yards and yards of pale green tiles. In consequence, the water looked smooth and inviting, and deliciously transparent.

The changing-rooms were comfortably equipped, and spacious. Each compartment had its own shower and vanity unit, and the pine-panelled walls gave the illusion of being in a cabin. Alex had left the selection of bathing-suits on the vanity table and, looking through them, Isabel realised they were all far more revealing than anything she might have chosen for herself. Still, she reflected, she hadn't bought a swimsuit for over a year, and the ones she had back at her apartment were probably out of date.

She eventually chose a one-piece *maillot,* that was mainly black, with inserts of blue and amber. It was the least vivid of all the swimsuits, but the amount of thigh exposed by its cut-away leg-line caused her some embarrassment as she walked out to find Alex.

He was already in the water. He had shed his polo shirt and was presently perfecting a slow crawl from one end of the pool to the other. But, as if some sixth sense had alerted him to her presence, he lifted his head and saw her and, abandoning his efforts, he swam swiftly towards her.

'What's wrong?' he asked, as her hands hovered protectively at the backs of her thighs, and Isabel cast her doubts aside.

'Nothing,' she said, as he folded his arms on the pool-side at her feet, realising she was only drawing attention to herself by behaving coyly. 'What's it like?'

'Come and find out,' he said, holding out his hand towards her, but she had more sense than to take it.

'In my own time,' she insisted, sitting down on the edge of the pool and dipping her feet into the water. 'God, it's freezing! I thought you said it was only fairly cool.'

'It is—once you're in,' he replied, turning on to his back and spreading his arms wide. 'Come on. It's beautiful!'

Overhead, a watery sun was trying to penetrate the low-hanging clouds, and the pool took on a glittering opacity. Luxury, indeed, she thought ruefully, finding it difficult to believe she was really here. Had she once taken all this for granted? Maybe if she'd been married to Alex, it wouldn't have seemed just a compensation.

Slipping off the rim of the pool, she allowed herself to slide down into the water. It was deeper than she remembered, easily four feet, even at this, the shallow end. Further along, where the water-slide and the diving-boards were situated, it was almost ten feet.

She was catching her breath when Alex swam back to her and, ignoring her efforts to evade him, he grabbed her hand and pulled her after him towards the middle of the pool. Pretty soon, she was out of her depth and compelled to swim or pull both of them down, and she panted indignantly as the chill of the water penetrated her skin.

'Are you trying to drown me?' she exclaimed, when he released her, and she was forced to tread water to keep afloat.

'You forget—I've seen you swimming,' he retorted, unmoved by her protests. 'Now—isn't this good? Much better than languishing in some stuffy restaurant all afternoon.'

Isabel sighed. 'Is that why——'

'Just enjoy it,' he overrode her insistently. 'No one's going to hurt you here. Not while I'm around, anyway. OK?'

It was difficult to do anything else but enjoy herself, with Alex doing everything in his power to help her. Chris had never used the pool much, and even when they were on their honeymoon, he had much preferred to sit at the pool-side bar, drinking daiquiris, to splashing about in the water. But Alex was different. He was an excellent swimmer, for one thing, and he evidently enjoyed the water as much as she did. So much so that the short dip she had envisaged lasted over an hour.

When she finally protested that she was too tired to swim any more and climbed out on to the side, her legs felt like jelly, and she flopped down on a padded air-bed, uncaring of what she looked like. After squeezing the moisture out of her braid, she rested back on her elbows, drawing up one leg in innocent provocation and tilting back her head to rest her aching muscles.

'You're out of condition,' Alex remarked, his shadow blotting out the shaft of sunlight in which she was lying. Opening her eyes, she saw he had vaulted out of the pool and was standing looking down at her, the shorts he had worn to swim in moulded to his thighs. 'You notice I don't say out of shape,' he added lazily. 'That wouldn't be true. You always were a beautiful woman, Isabel. On that score, Chris and I were always in total agreement.'

Isabel's inertia fled. It was the first time he had brought Chris's name into their conversation, and whether it had been deliberate or not, it had immediately destroyed her mood.

She sat up. 'I think I'd better get dressed,' she said, preparing to get up, but Alex's hand on her shoulder held her where she was.

'Not yet,' he said, hooking another of the cushioned air-beds towards them. Then, dropping down on to it, he faced her steadily. 'We have to talk.'

'To talk?' In spite of the water she had swallowed in the pool, Isabel's mouth felt suddenly dry. 'I don't think we have anything to talk about, Alex.'

'That's not the impression you've been giving me,' he remarked softly. 'You wanted to know why I brought you here. Don't you want me to tell you?'

Isabel lifted her shoulder to escape his touch, and he withdrew his hand at once, sitting cross-legged on the air bed beside her, apparently indifferent to the water trickling down his chest from his wet hair.

'I—thought you said it was to erase an unpleasant memory,' she countered tautly. Her lips twisted. 'Don't tell me it was to try and effect a reconciliation between me and Chris.'

'Why would I want to do that?' Alex was sardonic. 'I'm not that benevolent. Chris had his chance, and he blew it. I don't intend to do the same.'

Isabel swallowed. 'I don't know what you mean.'

'Oh, I think you do.' His eyes were disturbingly intent. 'In fact, I think you recognised it right from the beginning. You know, they say hatred is akin to love——'

'No!' Her heart palpitating wildly, Isabel tore her gaze away from his and scrambled to her feet. 'I don't have to listen to this. I'm going to get dressed.'

'Scared?' he queried, as she started towards the dressing-room, and because she resented his ability to see right through her, she halted.

'Not—scared,' she contradicted huskily. 'Amazed, perhaps. I never thought I'd see the impassive Mr Alex Seton reduced to speaking in clichés!'

His lips twitched, and turning, he rested back on his elbows to look up at her. 'I'm not impassive, Isabel,' he informed her wryly. 'Impatient, perhaps; frustrated, certainly. But not impassive. Not where you're concerned.'

She gasped. 'I don't believe this!'

'What don't you believe?'

'I don't believe you're saying what you're saying. Heavens, two days ago, you practically used court-room brutality to make me look a fool!'

'Not a fool,' he corrected her quietly. 'Just—ignorant of the facts, that's all. And I did apologise.'

'And that makes it right?'

'No.' He abandoned his lazy stance and sat up. 'It just attempts to explain the—ambivalence of my position.'

Isabel shook her head. 'Is that how you square your conscience?' she enquired scornfully. 'By calling your position ambivalent?'

Alex sighed, and with a lithe movement, he got to his feet. 'I couldn't—square my conscience, as you put it, even if I wanted to,' he said, a little more forcefully.

'And this isn't getting us anywhere——'

'Us?' she snorted.

'Yes, us,' he insisted, stepping off the air-bed and coming towards her. 'Isabel, you know what I'm talking about.'

Isabel took a step backward. 'No, I don't.'

'Yes, you do.' He considered his words before adding, 'Ever since I came to your apartment that first time, I haven't been able to touch another woman.'

Isabel's lips parted. 'And is that supposed to mean something?' she demanded. 'My God! Are you blaming me because you're temporarily impotent?'

Alex closed his eyes for a moment, and when he opened them again, she had put at least another three feet between them. 'Don't be crude, Isabel,' he said wearily. 'It doesn't suit you.'

'Well . . . ' She moved her shoulders nervously. 'What do you expect? Sympathy?'

Alex's mouth compressed. 'OK, OK.' He gave a careless shrug and turned away, 'If that's the way you want it, go ahead. Get dressed. I'll take a shower, and drive you back to town.'

'Wait!' The word sprang from her lips before she could prevent it, and although Alex hesitated, eventually he turned to look at her again.

'Well?'

Isabel licked her lips. 'Why—why did you invite me to have lunch with you?'

His brows arched. 'Do you really want to know, or are you getting ready with some other clever retort?'

She tried to control her breathing. 'I—really want to know.'

Alex stepped towards her. 'Because, in spite of everything I've said and done, you were right all along. I do want you. I think I always did.'

Isabel trembled. 'You mean—you mean——'

'I mean,' said Alex, removing the space between

them, 'that ever since I came into the library here and
found you with Chris, my feelings for you have never
been ambivalent.'

Isabel shook her head, the wet braid sending a
spray of drops across the tiled surround of the pool.
'But you hated me!' she protested.

'I said my feelings had never been ambivalent,' Alex
reminded her softly, stroking damp strands of hair
from her forehead with his thumbs. 'I did hate you
then; because you were marrying Chris. I hated him,
too, but that I could control.'

Isabel blinked, looking up at him disbelievingly.
'And—and that evening you drove me down from
London——'

'I think you know how I felt then,' he muttered,
bending his head to touch her bare shoulder with his
tongue. 'If that policeman hadn't interrupted us, I'd
have taken you there and then.'

Isabel quivered. 'I wish you had,' she whispered
fervently, as he drew her into his arms, and Alex said,
'So do I,' against the parted sweetness of her lips.

His kiss was firm and gentle, as Alex rediscovered
the contours of her mouth, a sensuous benediction to
the altar of her beauty. There was no rush, no haste,
no hurried need to satisfy the senses. Just a sensual
awakening to the delights that they might share. Even
the hands that caressed her waist made no overt
attempts to disconcert her. Alex was quite content to
explore her lips, her cheeks, the fluttering femininity
of her lashes, and the scented hollow behind her ear
with his tongue, so that by the time he found her
mouth again, she was aching for much more.

This time, when he kissed her, she responded,
urgently, winding her arms around his neck and
pressing herself against him. It was marvellous feeling
his hard body close to hers, and not until her breasts
encountered a certain roughness did she realise he had

pushed the strapless bodice of her swimsuit down to her waist.

'What—what if someone comes?' she stammered huskily, as his hands slid from her waist to find the swollen fullness of her breasts, and Alex's lips twisted.

'I don't particularly care,' he said honestly, lowering his lips to take one rose-tipped nipple into his mouth. 'But relax,' he added, as she jerked beneath his hands, 'no one will come.' He smiled. 'They wouldn't dare.'

'Are you sure?' she fretted, shifting her weight from one foot to the other, and with another lazy nod, Alex sought her mouth again.

'I'm sure,' he told her, cupping her face between his hands and rubbing his forehead against hers. 'Besides, we've got nothing to be ashamed of. You're not married this time.'

In spite of the lethargy that Alex's kisses were inducing in her, Isabel heard his careless words quite succinctly. 'This—this time?' she echoed blankly. 'Why—this time? I wasn't married when——'

'Forget it.'

Alex didn't want to talk right then, but Isabel's brain was clearing with every second that passed. 'When, Alex?' she pressed him urgently. 'When did we ever do this before? I was never unfaithful to Chris, ever! You know that. Don't you?'

Alex allowed her to escape only to arm's length. 'Well, not with me,' he conceded softly, his thumbs caressing her shoulder. 'Darling, it really doesn't mat——'

'It matters to me!' she exclaimed, and now she tore herself out of his grasp. 'You—you still believe it, don't you? You still believe I had an affair with Jerrold Palmer.'

Alex's shoulders sagged. 'Isabel, we don't have to talk about this——'

'We do!'

'Why?' He sighed. 'Look, I'm prepared to accept that you and Chris were not compatible. And, knowing how I feel about you, I'm even prepared to admit that, being the passionate woman you are, you needed someone else——'

'How big of you!' Isabel caught back the sob that trembled on her words. Alex still didn't believe her. He never had. He was prepared to make her his mistress believing she and Jerrold Palmer had been lovers!

'Isabel, Isabel . . . ' Alex was trying to reason with her. 'Don't you see! It doesn't matter to me. God, why do you think I stayed away from Nazeby so much after you and Chris were married? I knew you two weren't happy, and I was afraid that if I spent any time with you, I might destroy us both!'

Isabel was struggling to pull the *maillot* over her breasts. 'And I suppose I destroyed myself?' she choked, her fingers shaking so much she could hardly do anything, and with an oath of impatience, Alex stepped towards her.

'Here,' he said roughly, 'let me!' But Isabel was too strung up to let him touch her again.

'Keep back,' she said, jerking violently away from him, and as she did so, her foot slipped, and she pitched backwards into the water.

In normal circumstances, the fact of falling into the pool would have meant little. But in her present state, her hands shaking, and her breathing shallow, she was in no condition to weather the body-blow of the water. Instead, she gulped as the air was knocked out of her, and felt a stinging pain as water surged into her lungs.

She thought she must have lost consciousness, for she remembered little of the next fifteen minutes. She had a vague recollection of Alex hauling her out on to the pool-side and applying pressure on her back to clear her lungs, but it all had a dream-like quality.

Her first real coherency came when she was lowered on to the silky coolness of a bedspread, and the softness of a mattress eased the bruises from the pool-room floor.

She blinked and looked around her as another weight was deposited on the bed at her side, and she breathed a little less easily when she discovered that it was Alex.

'Wh—where am I?' The honey-brown walls and gold silk draperies were not familiar.

Alex grimaced. 'On a bed,' he said, and she noticed that he had shed his wet shorts in favour of a pair of cotton trousers. But his chest was still bare, and he looked distractingly handsome.

'I know that,' she said, feeling her throat ache a little when she swallowed. 'But whose bed? This isn't the room I was in before.'

'It's my bed, actually,' he informed her flatly. 'But don't worry, I'm not planning my revenge. I just thought you'd prefer not to have what happened broadcast. So I brought you up here to recuperate . . . '

Isabel caught her breath. 'But I'm wet.'

'Yes, you are.' He shrugged. 'I didn't think you'd approve if I changed your clothes.'

'I wouldn't.' Isabel propped herself up on her elbows and looked about her. 'Why didn't you put me on a towel? This swimsuit is going to ruin the bedspread.'

'I didn't want to,' said Alex honestly, smoothing the satin spread with a lazy hand. 'I wanted to see how you looked against my pillows. Putting you on a towel would have spoiled the whole effect.'

Isabel had never heard anything so erotic in her life, and in spite of the recklessness in doing so, she couldn't prevent herself from asking 'And?' in a voice husky with emotion.

Alex's dark eyes appraised her. 'I'd have preferred

you naked,' he said, with devastating candour, and
before she could escape, he had bent his head and
covered her mouth with his own.

It was not like his other kisses. This time, there was
a feverish urgency in his lips, and the tongue that
fought its way into her mouth was hot and sensual.
He wasn't just kissing her, she realised, he was giving
a fair impression of what it would be like if he
possessed her, and her protests wilted beneath the
hungry pressure of his mouth.

She lifted her hands to fasten them in the still-damp
thickness of his hair, determined to force his head
away from her; but she couldn't do it. Instead, her
hands slid compulsively round his neck, curling into
the silky hair at his nape, sliding up against his scalp
and pulling him down on top of her.

She managed a shaky 'Alex!' when she felt his
fingers in the bodice of her swimsuit, forcing it down
to her hips, but he didn't stop. This time, he pushed
the offending garment down to her ankles, following
its progress with his lips so that she was incapable of
resisting him.

Naked now, she gave herself up to the sensual
pleasure of his lovemaking. She was deaf and blind to
the dangers in what she was doing, and any doubts
she had were submerged by the simple needs he was
creating inside her. No one had ever kissed her, and
caressed her, and aroused her, as Alex was doing, and
what had always seemed so wrong with her emotions
suddenly seemed so right.

There seemed no part of her body he hadn't touched,
and although she knew he was on the bed beside her
now, she was hardly aware that he was naked, too.
Only the length of his legs rough against hers, alerted
her to their intimacy, but her mind was spinning so
dizzily with his kisses, she had no sense of inhibition.

'You're beautiful!' he groaned, burying his face

between her breasts, before cupping their fullness in
his hands and suckling them urgently. Her nipples
swelled and hardened beneath his searching tongue,
and she knew a sense of wonder at her own body's
fulfilment.

When he left her breasts to trail his lips down over
her waist and her flat stomach, she dug her nails into
his hair as if to stop him, but the erotic caress of his
tongue in her navel evoked even more pleasure. He
was sensitising every quivering muscle, and when he
reached the apex of her thighs, she shuddered convul-
sively.

'Now—I think . . . ' he said huskily, sliding back
over her, the throbbing heat of his arousal hard
against her stomach. With infinite tenderness, he parted
her legs to slide into her, and seconds before she felt
any pain, she knew the sensuous nudge of his manhood
against her.

Even then, she felt no urge to draw back, even if he
had been prepared to let her. This was what she
wanted; this was what she had been made for; and
there was no one else but Alex whom she wanted to
share it with her.

She realised she should have told him, the minute
he thrust himself inside her. She had thought she was
ready; that all those books she had read, which had
said it could be painful, were exaggerating. But they
weren't. She had not realised he was so big, or so
powerful. His unguarded invasion tore into her like a
knife, and although she tried to stifle her cry, Alex
was too experienced to doubt what he had done.

For seconds after he had buried himself inside her,
he lay completely still, and as the pain subsided, Isabel
began to hope she might get away with it yet. But
then, with a groan of anguish, Alex turned her face
up to him, and she saw his raw frustration that she
had deceived him yet again.

'You should have told me!' he bit out savagely, and although she knew she had tried to explain the truth many times, his total self-derision would not allow her to let him take the blame. Ignoring his instinctive attempt to propel himself up from her, she wound her arms round his neck and dragged him down to her again. With deliberate provocation, she slipped her tongue between his teeth and courted his participation. Then, when his teeth closed upon her tongue, to prevent its seductive dance, she let one hand trail down his back to his buttocks, and he groaned protestingly in his throat as his own needs overwhelmed him.

'Isabel . . . ' he muttered, as she ran one foot lightly up and down his calf, and she arched against him.

'I thought you wanted me,' she whispered, innocently, stroking his nipple with a delicate finger, and he closed his eyes.

'I do. I do!' he acknowledged tormentedly and, giving in to his emotions, he captured her lips with his . . .

CHAPTER ELEVEN

'YOU don't mean this, Isabel!' Jason stared at her disbelievingly, a look of frustration marring his faintly over-indulged features, and Isabel thought how typical it was that he should still assume he knew what was best for her.

'I do,' she insisted now, dropping down on to the chintz-covered sofa, and crossing one long, slender leg over the other. 'Jason, it's no use! I'll never go back to modelling.'

'Don't say that!' Jason sighed, spreading his hands. 'Isabel, when—when this is all over, you're going to feel altogether different, believe me. You'll soon get bored with this—*rustic* existence.'

'I don't think so.'

Isabel turned away from him to stare through the lattice windows of the cottage, out on to the fields that bordered the canal a hundred yards away. Somewhere a farmer was ploughing a furrow, preparing the soil for the winter's planting, and the steady drone of the tractor's engine was soothing. It helped to smooth away the disturbing ripples that Jason's invasion into her life here always created and, thinking of the changing seasons, she was more convinced than ever that this was where she would stay. Perhaps we do retain some remnant of our ancestry, she reflected ruefully. Certainly this corner of Norfolk, that bordered on Lincolnshire, seemed to hold some attachment for her. Or perhaps it was simply the fact that this cottage had been available, and she had leased it, she admitted honestly. And its distance—and inaccessibility—from London *had* suited her purpose.

Jason's nostrils flared. 'Don't you think you're being rather reckless? Something could go wrong. Situated like this—miles from anywhere—what happens if you're taken ill?'

'There is a phone,' said Isabel shortly, indicating the instrument occupying a corner of the window-ledge. But he had voiced a fear she had already experienced. In spite of her assertions of independence, her isolation here was a little daunting to someone used to city life. She wasn't afraid of being ill; she had always been disgustingly healthy, and in the last few weeks, that had not been one of her priorities. But being alone at night still made her nervous, and even the knowledge that the Vicarage was only a few yards away was no compensation in the middle of the night.

'Nevertheless,' Jason exclaimed now, 'sooner or later you're going to have to come back to town.' He made an impatient gesture. 'Won't you have to attend the Denby board meetings, at least sometimes?'

Isabel bent her head. 'As a matter of fact, I'm thinking of selling the shares.'

'Selling them!' Jason was astounded. 'After what you said!'

'I know, I know.' Isabel lifted her shoulders. 'But I don't want to see any of the Setons ever again, and by selling the shares, I can guarantee that.'

Jason snorted. 'You're a fool!'

'Maybe.'

'Robert Seton won't thank you for it.'

'I don't expect him to.'

'But you do intend giving him first option on the shares.'

'Probably.'

Jason shook his head. 'You're crazy! Put them on the open market. Let him bid for them, like anyone else.'

'I don't think Vinnie would have wanted that.'

'Vinnie!' Jason was scathing. 'I suppose you realise your precious Vinnie is responsible for everything that's happened. If she hadn't involved you in the company in the first place, you'd never have seen Alex Seton again.'

Isabel got to her feet now, a slim, defensive figure in her long suede skirt and loose-sleeved shirt. 'I'd really rather not talk about it,' she said, crossing the low-beamed room and disappearing into the adjoining kitchenette. 'Do you want some coffee? I'm afraid I've got nothing stronger.'

Jason seethed, but there was nothing he could do. Isabel had made up her mind, and he knew of old that nothing he said would change it.

'No,' he said now, pushing his hands into the pockets of his corded jacket. 'No, I've got to go. I've left some things at the hotel in Spalding, and I want to collect them before driving back to town.'

'Oh.' Isabel came to the door of the kitchen again, her slim hand resting against the frame. 'Well—thanks for coming.'

'My pleasure.' But Jason was ironic. 'Look after yourself, Isabel. Remember, if you change your mind, I'm just at the other end of the line.'

She kissed him then, going towards him and pressing her lips against his cheek. 'Thanks,' she murmured, her hand lingering against his lapel. 'I wish—I wish things could have been different.'

Jason grimaced. 'Yes. So do I,' he averred, putting her firmly from him. 'I'll be in touch. *Ciao!*'

She watched him drive away, the wheels of his Mercedes sending up a cloud of dust from the dry track. It was weeks since there had been any prolonged rain, and the lane from the cottage down to the main road was cracked and powdery. July had been a wet month, but both August and September had been dry, and now, at the beginning of October, the farmers were beginning to grumble about the drought.

Still, she reflected, glancing up at the overcast sky, perhaps their wishes were soon going to be granted. It certainly looked thundery, the clouds hanging on the horizon just lightly tinged with yellow.

Shrugging off the oppressive thought of an impending storm, Isabel went back into the cottage and closed the door. Then, she leaned back against its gnarled panels, acknowledging, somewhat ruefully, that Jason was unlikely to come again.

Since she had come to live at the cottage, he had visited her several times, always hoping, she knew, that time and isolation would bring her to her senses. But after today, after learning what she had had to tell him, he seemed finally convinced, and although she was relieved, she couldn't help a pang of remorse. He had been a good friend; better than she deserved. And maybe she would have second thoughts when the next six months were over.

But right now, the idea of going back to London, of possibly running into Alex again, and him learning what had happened, seemed no alternative at all. If things had been different; if she had still been seeing Alex, the situation might have had endless possibilities. But they weren't, and she wasn't and, thanks to Jason's co-operation, her secret would remain her own.

Leaving the door, she crossed the room to the fireplace, and added another log to those already smouldering there. The day wasn't exactly cold, but the cottage walls were thick, and even on the hottest day, a fire was not out of place. Besides, it heated the water, and although the plumbing was primitive, she intended to take a bath that evening.

She was feeling hungry, too, and, discovering it was half-past four, she decided to make herself some tea.

These days she felt hungry at the oddest times, and because she had only herself to please, she generally kept country hours.

She got most of her provisions in the village, only driving into Spalding when it was absolutely necessary. She knew the local people were curious about her, but she managed to keep herself to herself. The only person she had had a long conversation with was the Vicar, although she had confided in the doctor that she did have private means. If only to reassure her neighbours that she was not a fugitive criminal, she had excused herself afterwards. But the truth was, she didn't want anyone feeling sorry for her. A hangover from her childhood, no doubt, but important none the less.

She went for a walk after her tea. She did a lot of walking these days, and she was considering getting a dog. As well as the companionship it would offer, it would give her a reason for going out. A woman walking alone attracted all sorts of undesirable comments. Still, since coming to Norfolk, she had tackled her own housework again, and the idea of having an animal shedding hairs all over the furniture was not appealing. Maybe later, she decided, when she decided to buy a house.

It was almost dark by the time she got back, and she locked the door behind her, and quickly drew the curtains. It was another of her foibles that she never turned on the lights until the curtains were drawn. Living in the city had made her super-cautious.

However, with the curtains drawn against the night, and a low rumble of thunder echoing across the marshes, it was cosy in the cottage. She poked the fire into flame and turned on her radio, and then went out to the kitchen to prepare her bath.

It was one of the vagaries of the cottage that the bathroom was downstairs. Someone, a previous tenant

she guessed, had turned what used to be a larder into
a bathroom, and although the pipes were efficient, the
floor was made of stone. It was nothing like the
luxurious whirlpool bath she had at her apartment,
and she tried not to think of what it would be like in
winter as she rapidly shed her clothes.

Soaking in the claw-edged tub, though, she could
forget her surroundings. The warmth, the sudsy depth
of the water, was like a womb, cocooning her against
the world outside. As her womb was cocooning Alex's
baby, she acknowledged painfully. How strange it was
that although she never wanted to see the child's father
again, she already loved the scrap of humanity growing
inside her.

She sighed. Jason's appearances always coincided
with thoughts like these. Or rather, his arrival trig-
gered memories she would rather forget. After all, the
first time he had come, she had half expected Alex to
be with him. But each succeeding visit had taught her
the futility of that.

If only she knew what Alex had been thinking when
he had left for South America. Was it only coincidence
that he had left the day after their visit to Nazeby?
And why had he gone to South America anyway? It
wasn't as if he had any connection with his uncle's
business there.

She had racked her brains to try and find a solution,
but she had never found one. All she knew was that
Alex had gone away without seeing her again, and
that although she had waited almost three weeks for
him to get in touch with her, he hadn't.

She shook her head. She had thought—she had
really thought that discovering she had never slept
with any other man would prove to Alex that Chris
had been lying. It *must* have proved it; and to begin
with, she had believed he had gone to South America
to confront his uncle with that proof. But as the days

and weeks went by, without any further communication from him, she had to accept the inevitable: that although Alex had wanted her, her innocence didn't mean a thing.

And after all, he had virtually told her that, when he was kissing her down at the pool. Her outrage that he should have believed she had had an affair with Jerrold Palmer hadn't meant a thing to him. He had only been interested in her body, and although he hadn't liked the idea of her taking a lover at the time, the fact that that was all over—as he saw it—cancelled out any further recriminations.

She shook her head. She should have realised what he was like then, she acknowledged now. She should have known he was too much like his uncle to suddenly change character. He had wanted her, and he had had her—by fair means or foul—and once that was accomplished, he had no further interest.

A lump formed in her throat at the realisation that she would never see him again. No matter how determined she was not to let the memories hurt her, they always did, but with each succeeding day, she was becoming stronger. This time, she had even restrained herself from asking Jason if he had seen him. He had told her so many times, she had at last accepted the truth.

Alex had gone away, because it was the simplest method of severing any connection between them. He must have known that after that passionate interlude at Nazeby, she would want to see him again, and simply to leave the country saved a dozen bland excuses.

She sighed. Even now, there were occasions when she found it hard to believe that he had not got as much out of that afternoon as she had. He had seemed so sincere at the time, and the fervour of their lovemaking had lasted well into the evening. It was true, they had not talked much, but Isabel had been content that there would be time enough for talking afterwards. Just then, she had more important needs to be satisfied, and she had found herself insatiable when it came to loving him.

They had made love several times, and in between they had slept in each other's arms. They had only stirred to love again, and that first unfortunate experience had been erased by the ecstasy that came after. Alex was so good at it, she fretted now, feeling the familiar ache in the pit of her stomach that always came with thoughts of him. After her experiences with Chris, she had half believed herself to be frigid, but with Alex she had reached the heights again and again.

They had explored one another's bodies with a thoroughness she could hardly believe now. Alex had been totally without inhibition, letting her do with him as she willed. And she had lost all modesty beneath the possessive touch of his hands.

It was Mrs Cowie who had eventually disturbed them, knocking on Alex's door and asking if he was staying to dinner. Isabel had waited, hoping he would say they were staying the night, but he didn't. 'We'll have dinner back in town,' he had called to the housekeeper carelessly, and then had taken Isabel once again, with the woman's retreating footsteps still audible to their ears.

The journey back to town had been a strain for both of them. Isabel had not known what to say to bridge the gulf between their physical compatibility and their mental discord. It was difficult to imagine herself bringing up the subject of marriage, and it was equally illogical to avoid what must be said.

And then, when they got back to her apartment, when she was steeling herself to invite him in and get the whole thing over, she discovered Jason was waiting for her. He had finished the shoot earlier than planned,

he said, and feeling sorry for her for having missed
the trip, he had come to take her out to dinner. He
had been waiting around for over an hour, he added,
convinced that sooner or later she would turn up.
Isabel had had no choice but to invite him in in
consequence, and Alex had simply left her, with hardly
a word of farewell.

His message the next day was left on her answering
machine. It was short and almost lethal in its ability
to shock. He was leaving for Rio de Janeiro on the
morning flight. He'd get in touch with her on his
return.

Of course, he hadn't. Although she had known he
must be back in London, he had made no attempt to
contact her, and she had been too proud to contact
him. One week went by, then two; and by the third
she was already suspecting what had proved to be the
case. That crazy spate of lovemaking had left her
pregnant: after six desperate years she was going to
have a baby.

That was when she had decided to go away. At
first, she hadn't told Jason why; just that she and Alex
had had a brief relationship that had gone sour, and
that she needed some time to be alone.

And he had been surprisingly co-operative. She
suspected he didn't approve of her associating with
any member of her ex-husband's family, and he probably thought a few weeks' holiday would be enough
to solve her problem. He had had no idea that finding
this cottage on the borders of Lincolnshire would
prove so attractive. But by the end of August, he had
discovered her intention to give up modelling and,
since then, his enthusiasm had evaporated.

She hadn't told him about the baby until today;
and only then because he still refused to believe that
she was serious about giving up her career. Not that
he had accepted it entirely, she sighed. He probably

thought that once she had had the baby, she would rapidly come to her senses. Perhaps she would, she shrugged, and then ran a tentative hand over the faint swelling in her belly. But she didn't think so. Her child was not going to be abandoned by its mother; not if she had anything to do with it.

She was stepping out of the bath when she heard the rattle of the letter-box. She started first, and then relaxed, guessing it was the parish magazine, or some other circular they were delivering around the village. But when the noise came again, she realised someone was there.

Wrapping the towel closely around her, she padded silently through to the living-room, blessing her penchant for closing the curtains before putting on the light. No one could really know she was alone in the cottage. Not unless they knew her, she added, wishing that gave her more confidence. She had read too many stories about lonely women murdered by people who knew them. What did she really know about the people in the village? How well did she really know the Vicar?

'Isabel! Isabel, are you in there?'

The painfully familiar voice turned her knees to water, and she grasped the back of the sofa weakly, half inclined to believe she was hallucinating. *Alex!* Alex couldn't be here! It must be the Vicar, and she was superimposing Alex's voice over his cultured tones. That was it. It had to be. Alex didn't even know where she was.

'Mr—Baynes?' she said faintly, clutching the ends of the towel to her breasts, and there was a moment's silence before the voice spoke again.

'No,' it said, 'it's not *Mr Baynes;* it's Alex! For God's sake, open the door! There's an electric storm going on out here.'

She hesitated, torn by the desire to keep him waiting

while she put some clothes on, so that she could meet him on equal terms, and an equally strong concern that he might be struck by lightning. It wasn't that she cared for him, of course, she told herself, winding the towel about her. But she wouldn't like to have to call Mr Baynes to remove a dead body from her door-step. He was already curious why a young woman of her age and appearance should choose to bury herself in the wilds of Norfolk. If she had to explain her connection to Alex, she might well find herself head-lining the local newspaper.

'Isabel . . .'

'All right, all right, I'm coming!' she exclaimed, scurrying barefoot across the carpet. Reaching the door, she removed the bolt and turned the key, keeping herself hidden behind it as Alex strode into the cottage.

Closing the door behind him, she was absurdly conscious of her scant attire. It was all very well sitting in the bath, recalling that afternoon at Nazeby, and how intimate with each other they had been then. Now, it was three months since she had seen him, and what had been between them had long since lost its fire.

Alex had paused on the hearth, looking round her small domain with impatient eyes. Clearly, it was not what he had expected. She wondered if he had thought she had bought herself a house resembling his uncle's. With its occasionally smoking chimney and low beams, Marsh Cottage was no one's idea of luxury.

Then he turned to look at her, and she saw to her surprise that he looked tired. But it wasn't just that, she realised, her gaze dropping compulsively down the lean length of his body. He had lost weight, and his black suede trousers and leather jerkin could not hide the fact. How funny, she thought with bitter humour; he had lost it and she had gained it. There was a moral there somewhere, if only she could see it.

'Do I amuse you?' he asked, noticing her tilting lips and misinterpreting their meaning. 'If this is meant to be some kind of joke, do let me in on the punch line!'

Isabel rapidly sobered. 'What are you doing here, Alex?' she asked, straightening away from the door with unconscious hauteur. 'How did you know where to find me? Did you think of asking Jason at last?'

Alex's dark face was sombre. 'At last?' he queried harshly. 'Did I think of asking Ferry at last? It might interest you to know I've asked your photographer friend if he knew where you were on at least half a dozen occasions. But every time I got the same answer: don't ask, because *you* didn't want to see me.'

Isabel blinked. 'No!'

'What do you mean—no?'

'I mean—no, Jason wouldn't do that.'

'Wouldn't do what?' Alex sounded scathing. 'Keep your address from me? Oh, yes, he would. That bastard has it coming, believe me.'

'No, I   ' Isabel took a couple of steps towards him, biting her lips. She didn't understand this. Whenever she had asked Jason if he had heard from Alex, he had always said no. And she had believed him. Why wouldn't she? 'Jason . . . ' She stumbled to find the words. 'Are you saying you have asked Jason where I was?'

'In words of one syllable: yes.'

She blinked. 'But—why?'

'Why?' He sounded incredulous. 'Don't you know?'

Isabel stepped back again. 'There's been some mistake.'

'You bet your sweet life there has.' Alex was breathing heavily. 'And when I get my hands on Jason Ferry——'

'Oh, please!' Isabel shook her head. 'Don't talk like that. I—you must have said something to make Jason think you meant to harm me——'

'To harm you!' Alex stared at her savagely. 'My God! I think you've cornered the market on *harming* people! Or should I say one person; this person; *me!*'

Isabel shivered, but she wasn't really cold. She was just finding it incredibly difficult to accept the fact that Alex was standing here in her living-room, and what was more, he was saying that he'd been trying to find her. She dare not go beyond that. She had been hurt too much already.

'Are you cold?' he demanded now, turning to stare frustratedly at the smouldering logs. 'What do you do to get some heat around here? You'd better put some clothes on. This could take some time.'

'My—my dressing-gown's in the bathroom,' she said, unwilling to brave the stone floor again to get it. 'Behind you,' she added, when he looked up the stairs. 'The bathroom's off the kitchen. If you follow the steam, you'll find it.'

Alex hesitated, but then, with an impatient gesture, he strode out to the bathroom. 'Here,' he said, holding the green velour robe out to her. 'Drop the towel. I promise not to look.'

But he did. She knew it. Even though she turned her back, she could feel the penetration of his eyes through her shoulder-blades. And when she slipped her arms into the sleeves and drew it up around her shoulders, she felt him close behind her. The heat of his body was unmistakable.

'Thank you,' she got out at last, tying the belt of the robe about her waist and putting the width of the hearth between them. 'Um—can I get you a cup of coffee? I don't have any alcohol.'

'No?' His lips twisted. 'That's a pity. I could use a drink.'

'Well, then——'

'*Not* coffee,' he assured her grimly. 'Forget it. I can wait.'

Isabel pressed the heels of her hands together. 'If—if Jason didn't tell you where I was, how did you——?'

'I didn't say that,' Alex interrupted her. 'I said I'd asked him half a dozen times where you were and he wouldn't tell me. Today he had no choice. I cornered him in Spalding. I think he knew the game was over.'

Isabel shook her head. 'I don't believe it.'

'Don't? Or won't?'

She sighed. 'Why would he do it?'

'What? Keep me away?' Alex snorted. 'I guess he's jealous. I know the feeling, believe me.'

Isabel gasped. 'But—you went to Brazil!'

'Yes.' Alex nodded. 'The day after we went to Nazeby. Do you think I'd forget that?'

Isabel licked her lips. 'And—and when you came back you said you'd contact me.'

'Yes.'

She gulped. 'Well, you didn't.'

'Didn't what? Come back? I know. I can explain——'

'No——contact me,' she broke in huskily. 'You didn't contact me. I—I waited three weeks for you to ring, but you never did.'

'Not for three weeks, no,' he conceded heavily. 'Not for four, as a matter of fact. It's difficult to be confidential from the other side of the equator.'

Isabel stared at him. 'You mean—you were still in Brazil!'

'As you'd have found out, if you'd cared to ring my office.' Alex shrugged. 'I know I should have written. I did write on two occasions, but I destroyed the letters. I was afraid I'd read too much into our relationship, and no one was going to accuse me of being a fool a second time. When I got back and you'd disappeared, I was half inclined to believe that I'd been right.'

Isabel moistened her lips. 'I don't understand.'

'Well, that makes two of us,' he declared sardonically. 'Do you want me to explain, or am I making another mistake?'

Isabel shook her head. 'Just tell me what happened,' she whispered huskily. 'I want to know.'

'Why don't you sit down?' he said roughly, noticing how she was trembling, and Isabel subsided obediently on to the sofa. In truth, her legs did feel like jelly, and she wasn't sure how much longer they would have held her.

'OK.' Alex unzipped his leather jacket and pushed his hands into the pockets of his trousers. 'You won't like this, but the reason why I didn't ring you was because my uncle begged me not to. And, I thought I owed him that much, in spite of what he'd done.'

Isabel's eyes grew wary. 'You did what your uncle told you?' She swallowed. 'I see.'

'No, you don't see,' said Alex abruptly, squatting down in front of the hearth with a lithe, disturbing grace. 'Whatever you've thought of me in the past, when I flew out to Rio, it was to have it out with Robert Seton. I think I wanted to kill him; until I got there and discovered Chris had almost done it for me.'

Isabel frowned. 'Chris?'

'Yes, Chris,' said Alex, taking one of her hands and holding it between both of his. 'You know that affair with Palmer? The affair *I* accused *you* of having? Well,' he paused, 'Chris had got himself involved with someone in California, someone not as scrupulous as Palmer, someone who had taken pictures, and sent them to his father.'

Isabel caught her breath. 'You mean——'

'I think you know what I mean.' Alex bent his head. 'My uncle was being blackmailed for half a million dollars. The night I arrived in Rio, he had a serious stroke.'

'No!'

'Yes.'

'But there was nothing in the papers, no stories in the Press——'

'No. That was my job,' said Alex grimly. 'No one had to know what was going on or Chris would have become involved. Uncle Robert was scared to death that Chris would find out and exercise his right to take over the running of the company in his absence. Somehow, we managed to disguise his illness as heat exhaustion, until I could get him back to England.'

Isabel hesitated. 'And now? How is he now?'

'Partially paralysed,' said Alex flatly. 'He can speak, but not everyone can understand him. His doctor says he'll probably be confined to a wheelchair for the rest of his life. The trouble is, he's changed his will. Since—since that affair with Chris, he won't even agree to see him. He wants me to take over the running of Denby Industries, and I don't know what to do.'

Isabel gazed at him helplessly. 'Does Chris know?'

'About his father? Or about his father's will?'

'Well—both, I suppose.'

'Yes. He does now.'

'And?'

'Well, to begin with, he was pretty shattered; on both counts. Lately—well, lately, he's accepted it, I guess. In any event, he's considering moving permanently to the States. Apart from the unfortunate experience I mentioned, he likes it over there. He has friends in California, as well as enemies. He'll make out.'

Isabel's eyes were round. 'And the blackmailer? Did you have to pay the money?'

Alex's lips twisted. 'My uncle would have, I think. I contacted the police instead. They're pretty clued-in to cases like that. It was all sorted out with the minimum amount of publicity. He was a pretty amateur blackmailer.'

Isabel bit her lip. 'So that—that was why you couldn't contact me?'

'That was why.' Alex looked at her steadily. 'I knew you'd think I was all kinds of a heel, but what could I do? Until I got back to England, it was impossible. I just consoled myself with the thought that we had the rest of our lives ahead of us. Then, when I got back, you'd disappeared.'

'Oh, Alex . . . '

'And that bastard of a photographer wouldn't tell me where you were. Even today, he screwed me to get your address.'

'Screwed you?' Isabel blinked. 'I don't understand. What were you doing in Spalding anyway?'

'Would you believe—looking for you?'

'But——'

'Look, I've rung your apartment a hundred times, and I knew that creep was still seeing you. So——I had him followed. My contact said he'd lost him somewhere in Spalding yesterday. I drove up this morning and trailed round every estate agency in the town, showing them your picture. I was sure someone must remember you. You're not exactly unknown, you know.'

'I am here,' said Isabel ruefully. 'But when did you see Jason?'

'About two hours ago. He was coming out of an hotel with a suitcase. I cornered him, and he made up some story about checking out a location for a shoot. I think he realised I was likely to shoot him if he didn't tell me where you were. Anyway, after an argument, I agreed to let him submit terms for the spring catalogue at Denby Textiles, on condition he gave me your address. And here I am.'

Isabel caught her breath. 'He was interested in that

catalogue, as soon as he found out we were—related,' she exclaimed, and Alex pulled a wry face.

'So? What the hell! It was a small price to pay to find you. Just tell me that you wanted me to find you, and I'll consider it all worthwhile.'

Isabel quivered. 'Oh, Alex,' she breathed, leaning towards him and sliding her arms over his shoulders. 'I wanted you—so much!'

He moved then, subsiding on to the sofa beside her and pulling her hungrily into his arms. 'And I've wanted you,' he muttered, his mouth finding hers. 'I feel as if I've been serving a sentence, and you've just given me my freedom . . . '

It was some time before they spoke again, but when Alex aroused himself sufficiently to stir the logs to flame, Isabel smiled.

'I hope Mr Baynes doesn't come to call this evening,' she murmured, stroking caressing fingers down his spine. 'You're not exactly dressed to meet my neighbours, are you, darling? And I have the feeling he might not approve of what we've just been doing.'

Alex turned from the fire to look down at her. 'Who the hell is Mr Baynes?' he demanded, and her tongue appeared provocatively at his obvious impatience.

'Just the Vicar,' she said, too content to prolong her teasing. 'He's been quite a good friend to me, although I'm sure he thinks I'm in hiding.'

'You were,' Alex reminded her harshly, bending to caress her ear with his lips. 'My God, when I came home from South America, and discovered you'd disappeared, I nearly went out of my mind.'

'Did you?' Isabel looked at him as he lifted his head, sliding her fingers over his nape. 'But that night we drove back from Nazeby, you couldn't wait to get away.'

Alex groaned. 'That night we drove back from

Nazeby, I was too consumed by what had happened. I couldn't believe I'd been fooled for so long, and if I seemed remote, you have to remember, you'd thrown all my schemes for us aside.'

Isabel frowned: 'How?'

'Oh——' Alex sighed. 'After fighting my emotions for you for over six years, I'd finally decided to tell you how I felt about you. I was being magnanimous, you see. I'd managed to convince myself that my earlier resentment of your relationship with Chris had been justified by your *affair* with Palmer, but that whatever had happened in the past, we might still have a future together. I needed that justification, don't you see? Without it, I couldn't entirely banish the thought that I had *wasted* six years; that if I'd been honest about my feelings right from the start, you might never have married Chris.'

'Oh, Alex!'

'I know.' His hand curved possessively round her cheek. 'I've been a fool. I know that now. But that night I still needed a scapegoat, and Uncle Robert was it.'

Isabel's lids veiled her eyes. 'He—he knew.'

'I know that, too. Believe me, he didn't come off lightly. As soon as he was able to speak to me, I confronted him with it, and he had to admit that you had begged him to have the marriage annulled.'

Isabel trembled. 'He hates me. He always did.'

'*Hated,*' Alex amended roughly. 'He *hated* you. Right now, he doesn't hate anybody, and if I turned up tomorrow with you as my wife, he'd welcome you with open arms.'

'I doubt that.' Isabel blinked suddenly, and looked up at him. 'Wh—what did you say?'

Alex's lips curved. 'I said, if I turned up with you tomorrow, he'd welcome you with open arms.'

Isabel looked puzzled. 'But I thought——' She

licked her lips. 'Well, we'll have to see, won't we?'

Alex's laugh was teasing. 'Does that mean there's a doubt that you'll marry me?' he queried, and her eyes widened.

'Then—you did say——!'

'—that if I introduced you as my wife, my uncle wouldn't object?' He grinned. 'I may have done. Well? Do you want me to kneel?'

Isabel's arms imprisoned him on top of her. 'That won't be necessary,' she said huskily. 'Oh, Alex, I do love you!'

'Is that a yes or a no?' he murmured against her lips, and she hugged him closer.

'It's a yes,' she breathed unsteadily. 'Except—except there is one other thing . . . '

'I know.' Alex drew back to look down at her, and a faint colour invaded her cheeks.

'You know?'

Alex inclined his head. 'You're worried about me becoming chairman of Denby Industries,' he said softly. 'But nothing's definite yet. I told you. I don't know what to do about that. I wanted to talk to you about it, and we'll have plenty of time for that. If you don't want me to have anything to do with it——'

'That's not it.' Isabel broke into his words, expelling her breath on a long sigh. 'That is—well, whether you become chairman of Denby Industries is important, of course, but—there is something else.'

Alex frowned now. 'What else?' He hesitated. 'I've told you, Chris is leaving England——'

'It's not Chris.'

He shook his head. 'Then I don't know——' He looked puzzled. 'Unless you mean your shares. You can keep them——'

Isabel shook her head. 'Oh, Alex, it's not the shares. You can have them back, if you want. I'd already decided to offer them to you.'

'Then, if it's not the company—and it's not Chris
—and it's not the shares——' Alex gazed at her
uncomprehendingly. 'You're not—ill, or anything.
You're not hiding out here, because you thought I
wouldn't want you if I knew? Darling, if that's what
it is, we can find specialists——'

'I'm not ill.' Isabel allowed herself a broken laugh
now. 'Let me tell you! I—I'm pregnant. I'm going to
have a baby.'

'A baby!' Alex stared at her now, then his eyes
dropped lower, over the rosy fullness of her breasts to
the faintly discernible swell of her abdomen. 'Oh, God!
A baby! So that's why you hid yourself away up here!'

Isabel nodded. 'It was part of the reason, yes.'

'And the other part?' He was intent.

'You know the other part. Because I loved you, and
I couldn't bear to go on seeing you, thinking you
didn't love me.'

Alex's eyes darkened. 'Were you going to tell me?'

Isabel shook her head. 'I was afraid you might not
have believed it was yours.'

Alex groaned. 'Oh, love—*love!*' He buried his face
in the loosened glory of her hair. 'I believe it. I just
can't believe I've wasted so many years.'

'Well—perhaps we shouldn't waste any more,' she
ventured gently, spreading her palms over the smooth,
brown skin of his shoulders, and he agreed.

'Do you think this Mr Baynes of yours would marry
us?' he asked, his voice huskily teasing. 'As a newly
pregnant father, I'd like you to make an honest man
of me as soon as possible!'

Isabel smiled. 'You know, I wonder if Vinnie had
any of this in mind when she left me those shares,'
she tendered thoughtfully, and Alex drew her closer.

'You know,' he said wryly, 'you could be right. I
always thought the old lady was more perceptive than
the rest of us.'

Harlequin Presents

Coming Next Month

Available in January wherever paperback books are sold, or through Harlequin Reader Service:

In the U.S.
901 Fuhrmann Blvd.
P.O. Box 1397
Buffalo, N.Y. 14240-1397

In Canada
P.O. Box 603
Fort Erie, Ontario
L2A 5X3

Take 4 books
& a surprise gift
FREE

SPECIAL LIMITED-TIME OFFER

Mail to   **Harlequin Reader Service**®

In the U.S.
901 Fuhrmann Blvd.
P.O. Box 1394
Buffalo, N.Y. 14240-1394

In Canada
P.O. Box 609
Fort Erie, Ontario
L2A 5X3

YES!   Please send me 4 free Harlequin Romance® novels and my free surprise gift. Then send me 8 brand-new novels every month as they come off the presses. Bill me at the low price of $1.99 each*—an 11% saving off the retail price. There are no shipping, handling or other hidden costs. There is no minimum number of books I must purchase. I can always return a shipment and cancel at any time. Even if I never buy another book from Harlequin, the 4 free novels and the surprise gift are mine to keep forever. 118 BPR BP7F

*Plus 89¢ postage and handling per shipment in Canada.

Name	(PLEASE PRINT)
Address	Apt. No.
City	State/Prov. Zip/Postal Code

This offer is limited to one order per household and not valid to present subscribers. Price is subject to change.   DOR-SUB-1D

Readers rave about Harlequin American Romance!

" ...the best series of modern romances
I have read...great, exciting, stupendous,
wonderful."
                    –S.E.*, Coweta, Oklahoma

" ...they are absolutely fantastic...going to be
a smash hit and hard to keep on the
bookshelves."
                    –P.D., Easton, Pennsylvania

"The American line is great. I've enjoyed
every one I've read so far."
                    –W.M.K., Lansing, Illinois

" ...the best stories I have read in a long
time."
                    –R.H., Northport, New York

*Names available on request.

Harlequin
Intrigue

In October
Watch for the new look of

Harlequin Intrigue

. . . because romance can be quite an adventure!

Each time, Harlequin Intrigue brings you great stories, mixing a contemporary, sophisticated romance with the surprising twists and turns of a puzzler . . . romance with "something more."

Plus . . .
in next month's publications of Harlequin Intrigue we offer you the chance to win one of four mysterious and exciting weekends. Don't miss the opportunity! Read the October Harlequin Intrigues!